undertaking

what they didn't teach you

at mortuary school

Edited by
Stephanie K. Deal
&
Stacey Gilfus

NorGus Press
Auburn, New York

ISBN-10: 0615545823
ISBN-13: 978-0615545820

Printed in the USA by NorGus Press

Front Cover Photo © Eric Simard | Dreamstime.com
Back Cover Photo © Sergiy Rudenko | Dreamstime.com
Title Font is Sanctuary by Chad Savage | Sinisterfonts.com

Visit us online at www.norguspress.com

LETTERS FROM THE EDITORS

Every day when we got home from school the first thing we would do (after unsuccessfully raiding the refrigerator for sugar-laden snacks) was to turn on the TV. We only had four channels in my house during the early eighties, but four was plenty. Especially when one of those channels played reruns of Quincy, M.E. in the afternoon. It was a show that broke all kinds of barriers! Not only was it the predecessor to CSI, NCIS and many of other forensic shows with acronyms in its title, it proved that you can have a popular, gripping television drama starring an elderly leading actor who didn't possess "Hollywood beauty."

I would like to personally dedicate this book to the late, great Jack Klugman for capturing the attention of a teenage girl and keeping her overactive imagination delightfully entertained Monday thru Friday from 3 pm to 4 pm. To this day my curiosity still wants to know what was under the sheet that made all those police officers pass out during the opening credits.

~ Stephanie K. Deal

I love books. I love to read. Ever since I could pick up a book I've always had my nose buried in one. There is nothing I'd rather do than read a book. Amazingly, I now work with a great group of people to create books. I get to help choose, edit and format stories to create one of my favorite things. I found one more thing to love about books.

I would like to dedicate this book to my fellow NorGus publishers. Jeff, Matt, and of course my b.f. Steph. This one is for you. I appreciate the opportunity to work with you, to revel in your creativity, and of course have fun! What a great ride so far. Thank you my friends.

~ Stacey Gilfus

Other Anthologies from NorGus Press

Strange Tales of Horror
Look What I Found!

TABLE OF CONTENTS

DEAD TIRED
BY EMMA ENNIS

The steady stream of water drummed loudly on the glinting base of the stainless steel sink, the spray hitting the sides like whispers and dribbling wetly down the pristine white backsplash tiles on the wall behind. Adrian adjusted the temperature gingerly and tested it with a fingertip. That would suffice. He squirted some soap from the metal dispenser on the wall and lathered it between his hands, adding some water to augment the foam.

He leaned over the sink and splashed his face, the tepid water feeling heavenly against his tired, grimy skin. Standing up again, his chin dripping, he tore some paper towels from another clinical dispenser and patted himself dry. He turned off the tap and loosened his constricting tie, running still damp hands through his hair making it stand up in spikes.

He took one last glance around the room, ensuring everything was in order before he flicked the switch by the door and wearily climbed the stairs to the main house. On the landing he took a bunch of keys that hung on a nail and set about closing up the basement. The main lock snapped and he turned the key again, engaging the double lock, then moved on to the next one, and the next. He secured the security chain and, hanging the keys back on the nail, lifted the thick plank of wood that sat underneath and set it firmly in its slots on either side of the door.

His footsteps were muffled by the carpet as he made his way to the kitchen. He stopped halfway to remove his hard shoes, sighing with pleasure as his fatigued toes sunk into the thick pile, cushioning them like a new pair of slippers.

His wife Pam was standing by the stove, shovelling various delights from half a dozen steaming pots onto two already-heaped plates. He kissed her lingeringly on the cheek then sat at the table, glancing anxiously at the clock.

"Heavy day?" She asked sympathetically, laying his plate in front of him before slipping his jacket off his shoulders and draping it over the back of his chair.

"Dad was right when he said there is always work in the undertaker business." He answered vaguely.

After dinner they cleared up and then retired to the sitting room. While he spent his days below, making the money, his wife was busy making the house a home. The room was cosy; the perfect place to unwind after a hard day's work. But Adrian sat uneasily on the comfy cushions, his eyes darting periodically from the droning talk show host on the TV to the relentlessly ticking clock on the wall.

Eventually Pam stood up and stretched.

"Well, poke me I'm done." She stated, smiling cheekily.

Adrian smiled back, smacking her playfully on the bum.

"Coming up?" She asked, cocking her head towards the stairs.

He glanced at the clock again, his heart suddenly thumping.

"No I've got a few things left to do," he replied, trying to keep his voice even. "I'll be up shortly."

She pouted, though there was a hint of pity in her big brown eyes.

"Okay," she consented, brushing his hair back and kissing him on the forehead. "Don't stay up too late."

When the creaking of her nightly routines had ceased above him Adrian took his book from the side table; an insipid, frivolous work that he continued to drudge through just for the sake of it.

He hadn't gotten further than a few paragraphs when the words began to blur together and the delay between his blinks got shorter, the blinks themselves becoming longer with each one. The book slipped from his hand and fanned out in his lap. His head rolled to the side and was caught lovingly by the plump cushions. His mouth fell open and his breath came in long, even gusts.

A light tapping sound started up from somewhere underneath his feet, gradually increasing in momentum and intensity until it became a full force barrage, rocking the stillness of the sleeping house. Above the din rose a spine chilling moan. It rolled through the house, filling every nook with its resonance. It flowed down the hall and across the sitting room to where Adrian dozed on the sofa.

He sat up with a jerk, his eyes snapping again to the clock. His book slipped off his knee and clattered to the floor, startling him a second time. He stood up quickly and made his way to the kitchen, hitting the switch of the coffee machine with unwarranted force.

The foul liquid gurgled into his cup and he sipped it warily as he crossed the room to the phone table, his forehead crinkling with distaste. He hated coffee; loved the smell, detested the taste. A black appointment book lay open on the table and he flicked to the following day. His heart sank when he saw the lines of engagements that were scribbled there in varying shades of blue ink. There were three bodies coming to him from the city morgue in the morning *and* he had a meeting with a potential client who was debating having her dearest beloved interred by Adrian.

He looked at the steaming cup with regret before setting it down with a heavy sigh. He must go to bed. He did his rounds of the ground floor, flicking off lights and putting every second window on the latch so the air wouldn't be too stuffy when they got up in the morning. He took a glance at the basement door before proceeding upstairs. The chain had come loose and he replaced it with a shiver.

Reaching into the cubbyhole under the stairs he pulled out a dented baseball bat. He swung it once experimentally then took it with him upstairs and into the bedroom, where he crept quietly towards the bed in the darkness.

He tossed his clothes onto the chair and slid under the

covers, snuggling up close to his wife's soft, warm back. He kissed her cool shoulder before drawing the blanket over it. She was already deep in sleep, dreaming her peaceful sweet dreams. They had not gone to bed at the same time in years, not since he had started the undertaking business in the basement. That was something they didn't train you for in undertaker school.

Adrian was shattered but still he was reluctant to close his eyes. He lay in the darkness, fighting to keep them open, listening to the lonely ticking of the clock getting louder with every second that passed. Finally, when it felt like little lead weights had been attached individually to his eyelashes, he couldn't hold out any longer.

He gave his wife a final squeeze and kissed the back of her head through her silky hair. She shifted and snuggled tighter into him, her fingers groping in the darkness and finding his, entwined with them. The warmth from her touch spread through him and he sighed contentedly. He nestled into her hair. His eyes slid closed and almost willingly he drifted off to sleep.

The house settled creakily around its sleeping occupants. Across the street a dog started to bark, but whatever curiosity had alerted him was soon satisfied and he too snuggled down in his cosy kennel. A slight breeze took up, catching a stray newspaper sheet and pasting it against the garden fence where it fluttered between the posts for a moment before the little squall wandered off on its merry way and the paper fell and settled with a sigh on the footpath.

Inside the house, deep in the bowels of the basement there was a metallic clatter as some malignant looking tools slipped off the moveable work tray. A car passed on the street and the headlights momentarily beamed through the tiny excuse for a window. Shadows played over the black body bag that lay on a steel gurney in the corner, perhaps creating the illusion that it was moving. By some unknown force the tray tipped in the darkness and the rest of the tools slid to the floor, followed by the tray itself.

Upstairs Adrian shifted in the bed, the noise not quite waking him, but dragging him fitfully closer to consciousness. A series of thuds made him toss onto his back, still stubbornly clinging to the last dregs of sleep. There was an angry snarling sound. A rhythmic beat started, like heavy footsteps on wooden stairs, and then the door to the basement began to rattle, the chain jingling against the doorjamb, the deadbolt straining against the force that increased by the second.

Adrian sat bolt upright in the bed, his heart hammering in his chest just as the door downstairs banged against its restraints. A fevered howling sound broke above the clamour and faded, a chorus of deep, vibrating groans taking its place. Adrian swallowed hard. Here it comes. He reached over the side of the bed and felt around for the bat.

With his free hand he shook his wife, shaking more frantically when she refused to acknowledge him. Eventually she opened her eyes, ready to attack him for disturbing her, but he put his finger to his lips, signalling for her to be quiet.

"They're back." He whispered.

They clambered out of the bed and shuffled hastily towards the ensuite. He wouldn't allow her to turn on the light, practically slapping her hand away from the switch when she reached for it.

"I think they might be attracted to the light." He explained. Her eyes were wide in the diffused glow from the streetlamps.

Adrian placed his hand on her cheek for a second, then slid it around to the back of her neck and pulled her to him, crushing her lips with a fierce kiss.

"Lock the door after me." He whispered urgently as the sound of splintering wood echoed up the stairs, "Do *not* come out, no matter what, okay?"

He could see that she was about to protest but he stared her down. Still he had to prise her fingers from his so he could step back into the bedroom. They looked at each other once more – there were tears in her eyes – then he closed the door and waited until he heard the lock snap into place.

There was a big beast of a chest of drawers against the wall to his right and he heaved it in front of the bathroom door. They wouldn't take her. Not that night. He left the room, locking the door behind him – a useless precaution but at least it might slow them down.

He strode down the stairs but before he went to the basement he hurried in the opposite direction, flicking on all the lights in the rooms furthest from the stairs. If his theory was correct then that might draw them away from Pam. Taking a deep breath, he walked back down the hallway and stopped at the end of the stairs.

The basement door was dead ahead of him. It shook and rattled in its frame. The chain had snapped and the wood around the locks was cracked and would not hold out much longer. Adrian planted himself on the bottom step, gripping the bat in both hands, and waited.

The hammering grew in intensity, filling his head until he thought it was going to explode. Then the locks gave way and the door slammed against the deadbolt. The dreadful moans grew louder and a mouldy hand slipped through the gap. As though it had set off a chain reaction, more and more hands began to slide through, pushing and prising, straining against the barricade.

A cold sweat broke out on Adrian's brow. His hands felt slippery on the bat and he hastily rubbed them against his t-shirt just before the barrier snapped in half and the door crashed to the floor, inches from his feet.

The moans filled the air, a constant vibration that caused his teeth to rattle. The mouths that emitted them did nothing to ease his tension. Scores of hideous beings stumbled towards him from the basement, their bodies in various stages of decay. They were dressed like humans, formed like humans, but the eyes were dead and soulless, the mouths deathly weapons that were open wide, ready to latch onto anything living that came close.

Adrian held the bat high, gripping it so tight he could feel his knuckles straining. He stepped off the stair and swung the weapon with all he had inside him. It connected dully with fleshy bone, the shock of it travelled up his arm. The victim's groan ended in an 'oof' of surprise. Its head flew to the side and there was a loud snap as its neck severed from its spine.

The thing seemed to hang in the air for a moment before it fell back heavily, knocking against those behind him and sending them sailing down the stairs. Adrian could hear the thumps and cracks as numerous frail, chalky limbs were broken. But still they came.

Those that hadn't been knocked backwards simply stepped over those who had fallen, trampling their fellows underfoot. Adrian swung again and again, his shirt soaked with perspiration. A pile of bodies rose at his feet, innumerable groping hands breaking the wall, their owners felled in the act of grabbing for him.

More and more clambered towards him and he kept on swinging. The bat was coated in a bloody goo, bits of what looked distinctly like brain matter adhering to the tip.

A big fat man came for him, his grey flesh hanging in loose jowls as though it had become too heavy for his bones to hold. His mouth was open crookedly, his jaw broken. His fleshless fingers reached for Adrian and he recoiled, lashing out with the bat with all his might. It smashed into the skull and he heard a crack as the bat splintered.

He stabbed wildly with the jagged end but it was swallowed up in the saggy flesh and sucked from his grip. He turned and ran to the sitting room, grabbing the poker from the companion set which clattered onto the hearth. He spun to wait for them, weapon at the ready.

What was taking so long? He could hear their groans and wails but they did not seem to be following him. He inched to the door and was dismayed to see that a stream of monsters was already halfway up the stairs.

"No!" He yelled, bolting across the hall and launching himself over the banister into their path.

He attacked and stabbed like a man possessed, but for each one that fell two more took their place and he was forced further up the stairs. On the landing he glanced around wildly. His bedroom, and Pam, was down the hall to the left. He had two choices: he could try to lead them in a different direction, or he could retreat to the room and try to defend her from there.

He hastily decided on the former and started to back down the hall, away from the bedroom. He screamed when a set of stinking arms closed around his neck, trying to drag him to the ground. He wriggled from the hold, bringing the poker up and driving it forward. It sunk in the stomach of his attacker with a sickening squelch, and he twisted it for good measure before yanking it out again.

He had no idea how they had gotten behind him, but his meagre choice had now been whittled down to one so he turned and ran to the bedroom. Shoving the key in the door with trembling hands, he unlocked it and squeezed inside. He felt desperate fingers scrabbling at his back and didn't know if it was real or just his imagination playing tricks on him, fuelled on by his mounting terror.

Slamming the door behind him and locking it again, he went to the bed and shoved it away from the wall until the foot was against the door that was already beginning to shake in its latches. He bent down and with inhuman strength, heaved it up and stood it on its end. That ought to slow them down a bit.

From the bathroom he could hear terrified sobs, but as loud as they were they could barely rise above the hideous, ear-piercing screeches coming from the hall. The bed was beginning to teeter, rocking with the force of the blows on the door. He sprang to the bathroom door.

"Pam, love, let me in." He whispered, caressing the

wood as though it was a direct link to her.

The door opened and a frightened face peered cautiously through the crack. He pushed his way through. His eyes scanned the room but there was nothing of any weight that could be used as a barricade. In desperation he put the laundry basket against the door and stacked the bin on top, for all the good they would do.

In the bedroom there was a crash and rattle of springs as the bed fell and the door smashed in. Adrian looked to the shower cubicle. How long could that hold up? He glanced at the window. Would she survive the drop? What if there were more of them outside?

He turned to her. She was watching him, waiting for him to come up with the master plan that would save them. But he had nothing. They had reached a dead end. He put his hands on her shoulders, trying to think of something to say. *No.* He would not give up. Not again. They would take their chances with the window.

There was a deafening crack and the top panel in the door was ripped out. Swarms of zombies filled the room beyond, their grey, dead faces filling the hole in the door. Adrian made to shove Pam out of the way but it was too late. The grappling hands had her, clawing at her hair, dragging her top half through the opening while her bottom half remained in the bathroom with him.

Her screams froze his veins. He jabbed the poker into the faces surrounding her, but there were too many of them. A scraggy-haired female, her chin bloody where she had chewed away her own lip, bent her face to Pam's neck and sunk her teeth in. She let out a blood-curdling cry as the dead woman jerked her head back, grinning triumphantly around a mouthful of his wife's flesh. Pam's screams turned to a watery gurgle. Adrian stabbed and pushed but the poker was ripped away from him and he began to punch with his bare hands.

Another zombie latched onto Pam's cheek, tearing the skin from her bones. She was unable to cry out any longer, but her eyes pleaded with Adrian, begging him to end the pain. He roared in anguish, hot tears flowing down his cheeks as he struggled in the tug-o-war for his wife.

"Adrian." She whispered, her hand reaching for him, coming to rest weakly on his face. "Adrian wake up."

He couldn't let her die like that. She wouldn't end up on his table in the basement. Not his Pam. He... *wake up?*

His eyes cleared and the moans and screeches were replaced by a delicious silence. He looked around him. He was standing in the bathroom. The door was open, but it was intact against the wall. The bedroom beyond was empty. There were heart-wrenching sobs coming from somewhere and it was several seconds before he realised they were his own.

Pam stood at his shoulder whispering soothing words in his ear. He bundled her into his arms, still sobbing. He kissed her beautiful cheek, then buried his face in her neck, his salty tears wetting her soft skin.

Every night for six years. Every night they came and every night they made him a widower. Each time he struggled to keep her alive, hoping that if just once he could achieve this then the dreams would leave them alone.

That was something you could not train for at undertaker school.

THE WATCHER
BY JENNIFER L. BARNES

"She's late."

The gruff statement caused steam to curl up the damp, wet air as the icy drizzle continued to spill from the heavens. There were three figures dressed in white lab coats with stethoscopes huddled under a lit awning as they waited. The speaker pulled a pack of Marlboro reds from his scrubs, smacked it idly against his hip before pulling the golden twine to open it. One slender white stick emerged from the pack before being sealed and redeposited in its hiding place. The same hand reached into the opposite pocket and pulled out a cheap plastic lighter.

Yellowed teeth clamped on to the golden-brown end of the cigarette as fingers fumbled with the lighter. Sparks flew but didn't catch. "Goddamn it," he swore as he glared at the useless lighter, "Anyone else got a light?"

"Maybe it's a sign that you should quit," the youngest of the three wearing a shorter lab coat said with a grin. The smoker glared at him, but looked over to their one female companion, a stocky, middle aged woman with short mousy hair.

She grinned and said, "Here I come to your rescue as always, Bruce." A pudgy hand with only a white metal band adorning the ring finger reached into the pocket of her slacks. With a grin, she produced a simple steel Zippo lighter which she deftly snapped open, pressed her thumb down and fire erupted in a steady orange and yellow line. Bruce cupped his hands around his precious cigarette as she lifted the flame up to light it. Within moments, paper, tobacco and countless additives sparked red and then smoke curled up in a pale grey eddy to the sky, the light from the hospital catching it.

Bruce sighed and said, "Thanks Joyce, you're always a

godsend."

"No, I just know how much of a bitch you can be without your fix. Surprising that someone with a medical degree has a pack-and-a-half-a-day habit," Joyce said with a sigh and a shake of her head.

Bruce snorted and said, "If I was an actual sawbones instead of working with fucking dead people all the time I might be more careful."

"I'd figured since you worked with the dead all the time you'd do a better job taking care of yourself," the youngest said with a grin.

Dark eyes narrowed at the kid and Bruce said, "Price, shut the hell up." He looked down at his watch and asked, "Where the fuck is she anyway? If she waits too much longer then they'll wake up."

"We don't even know if they'll wake up," Joyce said in a firm voice as she pushed her glasses more firmly up her nose.

Bruce shook his head and said, "No Joyce, they always wake up."

"Technically they have about a seventy-five chance to wake up," Price said quietly.

Again the older doctor glared and said, "Most of the time, they wake up. You'll learn that soon enough kid. Jesus, why do we have to be babysitting, Joyce?"

"Because most med students don't want to keep watch. The money is finding a cure, not keeping track of the dead," Joyce said with a sweet smile.

Lips curled around the cigarette before a furious puff of smoke drifted heaven wards. "Fucking zombies."

Ryan Price sighed as Dr. Bruce Snyder let out another gust of cursing and cigarette smoke. The med student rolled up his sleeve to look at his watch. With a press of a button, aquamarine light appeared from the face revealing that the person they had been waiting for was only five minutes late. Considering the weather and traffic downtown this time of day it wasn't surprising.

"If we keep waiting they're going to get up and then they'll start eating people and then we'll get more of those fucking meat sacks," Bruce grumbled as the cigarette finally blew itself to a stub. It was extracted by crooked fingers, slammed into the stone wall of the hospital before meeting its final resting place in the stainless free standing ashtray outside the door.

The basement back entrance was used mainly for dead bodies. Living patents were brought in either through the roof by helicopter, the side bays or the front door. There was a reinforced room to keep dead bodies in case they truly weren't dead and rose. Unfortunately St. Mary's didn't have the budget for the government regulated gurneys with straps to keep newly risen zombies in place. Most of the time procedure called for some sort of head trauma to be given to bodies dropped off at the morgue to keep them from rising.

However there were occasions were that wasn't true. There were people for reasons religious or otherwise who paid insane amounts of money to keep from having their body "desecrated" before burial. If they woke up as zombies they would have to be dealt with, but they were monitored for a twenty-four hour period to make sure they didn't rise. Since the hospital didn't have the funds to buy the required restraining materials needed for keeping the dead in place if they woke up, they had to call in a specialist.

When the zombie threat reared its ugly head six years ago the world had almost been forced into an apocalypse due to the scourge of flesh eating ghouls. Just like in the movies, people who were bit by the zombies would turn into one themselves within a matter of hours. Well, half of the population anyway. After the initial onslaught had been curbed and the world's population dropping from over six billion to three and a half billion, research had gone on to find out what caused the Z-Plague as it became known as.

A Scottish virologist found that it was some rare retrovirus that had been excavated in a research mission in Greenland. Dr. Wallace had also found that half of the population had no defense against the virus and would contract it within hours after being bitten. It had also been discovered that about forty-five percent of the population would not contract the virus if bitten, but they were carriers. To subdue the rate of infection if one of the carriers were bitten they were sent off to colonies were they couldn't pass the infection on by exchange of bodily fluid. That act had been passed after a woman had been bitten by a zombie, showed no signs of infection only to have unprotected sex and have her partner become infected. Her partner did not have the normal incubation period of the virus like most victims, it took him longer to be infected and he had turned while in a crowded restaurant.

Then there were the remaining five percent that were immune and could not carry the virus at all. No one knew why this five percent were perfectly immune to the virus but tests were still being run to figure out what Rh factor in their DNA kept them from being infected. Since they were perfectly immune this five percent either helped in research to find a cure or became Watchers, task forces entrusted with dealing with outbreaks of zombies.

A loud rumble of an engine that wasn't an ambulance's plowed through the alley entrance. Bright halogen lights flushed pale blue then white as the vehicle got closer. Ryan shielded his eyes as he heard Bruce curse loudly. The lights died down and parked in front of them was a pristine, black new model Camaro. A blue jeans clad leg wearing knee high steel toed biker boots swung out of the driver's side.

"About fucking time that she got here," Bruce said as the figure stepped out of the car, shut the door and pressed a button on her key chain. The muscle car chirped once in acceptance, lit up and went dark again in response to its mistress's commands.

Standing there was a short, if somewhat stocky girl with dark hair pulled up into a pony tail wearing an armored motorcycle jacket and a black T-shirt. Apple green eyes fixed onto Ryan from a heart shaped face with plump cheeks. Bruce blew smoke and walked over to her. "You're ten minutes late, you know."

The girl's face twisted before she twisted her head to the side. Her short body bent forward as she started to cough loudly and violently. Small hands with the nails painted the color of gunmetal fumbled with one of the pockets of the heavy jacket only to retrieve a rescue inhaler. The cap to the inhaler was snapped off with one motion before the tube was shook heavily. Lips wrapped around the mouth piece as her thumb pressed it in twice, the hiss of the medicine accompanied by deep, whistling breaths.

She stood up to her full height before turning her head and coughing again. Her back was turned as Ryan flinched at the rasping cough of phlegm being brought up from the girl's throat. Within moments she turned back to them, her eyes red rimmed and watering before glaring at Bruce.

"I hate that fucking thing," she said in a low, husky voice as she glared at the inhaler before looking at Bruce. "Put out the fucking cigarette, jerk ass."

Ryan felt laughter bubbling up from within as Bruce's face seemed to melt. However the cigarette was still lit and still firmly in place in his mouth. The Watcher glared as she walked to the back of the car and said, "Look, I hate taking hits of my fucking inhaler before I have to do a job."

"Because it makes you shake," Joyce said with a worried frown.

She nodded, the dark pony tail swinging back and forth like a banner as she said, "Yeah, you try swinging an axe while having to deal with albuterol shakes. It's not fun times for anyone." She popped open the trunk and brought out an axe with a long shaft wrapped in black leather.

Bruce frowned and asked, "Aren't you suppose to have a gun?"

"Paging Doctor Dumbass, even a Watcher of the Dead shouldn't be bringing firearms into a hospital. Tends to make people panic, and people panicking around potential zombies means potential epidemic, got me?" she said with a scowl, "Plus, an axe doesn't run out of bullets."

The elder doctor's expression became more and more comical as he floundered at the sarcastic Watcher. A bright red flush spread across his already ruddy skin and his eyes began to bulge. To prevent total meltdown, Ryan stepped forward and held out his hand to her. He smiled and said, "I'm Ryan Price."

"Kristina Campbell," she said with a smile, flashing dimples in her rounded cheeks and green eyes sparkling. Her hand took his with a surprising grip and on second inspection he could see the tautness of her stomach even through the simple black T-shirt she wore.

Joyce held out her hand as well and said, "I'm Dr. Joyce Procter, and the chimney is Dr. Bruce Snyder. Ryan's a med student."

Kristina nodded and shook Joyce's hand as well, "Well, call me Kris. So, where are our potential meat bags?"

"Downstairs in a locked room by the morgue," Bruce answered in a gruff voice as he flicked his second cigarette into the standing ashtray.

Small hands lifted up to tighten the dark pony tail higher on her head as Kris answered in a drawl, "And they're unrestrained."

"And why do you think we had to call you, waste our time waiting for you to pull up in your showy car and bear with your disrespect?" Bruce asked with a look that was more gritted teeth than a smirk.

The Watcher shrugged and said, "It's not my fault that

your head slights you all the money to keep from getting a few reinforced gurneys." She flashed a lopsided grin and said, "It does mean I get paid extra though. So, let's see if the dead are going to rise tonight."

Her heart was currently doing a mighty jig against her ribcage and she had to fist her shaking left hand into her pocket while using her right to keep her axe balanced on her shoulder. Kris *hated* the tremors the rescue inhaler induced even after all of these years. Taking handfuls of pills a day she could handle, she could also handle injections, but she would have loved nothing more than giving her rescue inhaler a one way trip ticket to Hell never to be seen again. However much she hated her inhaler, she needed it to keep breathing when the people around her stupid and inconsiderate, much like the good doctor Snyder.

The two doctors were at the front of the group and Ryan the Cute Med Student was at her side, flashing her smiles, the hint of a dimple in his left cheek and bright blue eyes. He had hair the color of a startled carrot and was tall in that lanky sort of way that made him slump ever so slightly because all that extra height probably happened at once. She understood all too well what it was like to be self-conscious because of the way they looked a few years ago. Despite the guns she was rocking in her arms and the six pack currently engraved into her stomach she still saw the chubby high school girl who's asthma and steroids medication kept her from being svelte.

Of course a near zombie apocalypse is also good for one's physique, she thought dryly as she readjusted her grip on her axe.

Ryan smiled and asked, "So, how long have you been a

Watcher?"

"Since high school almost," she answered as they walked deeper and deeper into the hospital. That cloying smell of cleaners and fake oranges was starting to make her nostrils burn. The cough lodged quickly in her throat and she pulled her left hand out to stifle it. She swallowed and made a slight face at that oh-so-familiar salty, sickly bitter taste of phlegm as she fiercely pushed the lump back down her throat.

Her eyes darted around as they started to reach a few random desks. On one of the desks there was a leaning tower of text books with bits of paper sticking up through them. A brave pencil was resting precariously along the fold of the spine of one of the books where one false move could send it careening to oblivion onto the floor never to be seen again. Her chest tightened in a way that had nothing to do with inhaled chemicals or asthma.

That could have been me, she thought sadly as she passed by the desk.

"Really, you started that young?" he asked with wide eyes.

She raised her eyebrows at him and answered in a droll voice, "Well, you wise up really quickly when your whole class becomes card carrying members of the undead."

"What?" Ryan asked with wide eyes as he stared at her.

Wordlessly Snyder opened the door and she walked in. She turned towards the med student, smirked, and said, "George Romero couldn't prepare me for that day, let me tell you." Then, without a word she closed the heavy steel door before looking towards her charges.

"Look at the fat, wheezy nerd, puffing at her inhaler."

Kris clutched the strap of her backpack as her heart was pounding from the latest puff of the accursed inhaler. The red apparatus was deftly and swiftly slid in the recesses of her jeans before she turned around. One hand gripped her backpack as the shakes started to make her quiver while the other was deftly tucked into the same pocket as the inhaler. Her eyes narrowed as she looked at them, five in number and all taller than her.

Of course they were all boys.

Shouldn't there be some like unwritten rule in the code of manliness where it's penalty of castration to pick on a girl half your size? *Kris thought with gritted teeth as her heart was mimicking one of Lars' drum solos. One of them drifted up to her, his face pockmarked by giant pustules filled with a thick, yellow substance that threatened to erupt from his face at any given moment. He leaned closer to her and asked, "Is that the good shit, Campbell?"*

Breath redolent of things like chewing tobacco and other unsavory elements caused her to recoil with a grimace. She waved her hand in front of her face and retorted, "God, King ever heard of Orbit? You sure as hell could use a pack."

"You think you're fucking funny, Campbell?" a low, slow voice said from behind her as she was suddenly pitched forward.

Luckily being short and stocky kept her from falling on her face as she whirled around to face her attacker. Tall, broad shouldered and with a barrel chest stood Kris' personal nightmare made flesh. Saliva passed down her throat hard as she looked up at the one who had taken the attacking from verbal to physical. Pale, near colorless eyes looked down at her as he reached out a hand to shove her shoulder. She threw her weight into her thighs to keep from moving back as her eyes automatically looked around.

She replied, "I'm fucking hilarious, Skipp." Her chest tightened as her throat seemed to constrict, even with the recent puff she was trying to squeeze air into her firing lungs. A rattling cough escaped her throat and she pulled her forearm over her mouth.

"God, listen to you. What a fucking waste," Skipp replied moving to shove her again.

She started to move away, but King's bulk interrupted her flight. "Fat, wheezing, huffing at her inhaler, thinking she's better than us," King snorted as he gripped her shoulders.

Skipp smiled and said, "I wanna see what happens when she doesn't have her inhaler." His large, meaty hands began to reach for her and she tried to jerk away, but King held her fast. She looked around the hallway and only saw brick walls and some of the random skater kids staying as far away as possible, but keeping their voyeurs' gaze on the scene playing out before them.

One of guys in the group, a spindly youth who was always quiet during King and Skipp's sadistic games, started to pitch back and forth. His skin was faintly grey and was slick with sweat; his AC/DC shirt sticking wetly to his skin. Filmy eyes rolled up into his head before he groaned and collapsed to his knees. One skeletal hand reached up to grab Skipp's arm as a low moan escaped his lips.

Skipp spun around, his colorless eyes widening as his friend dropped before him. "Holy shit, Dean . . ." Skipp said as he started to help his friend to his feet.

The hands around Kris' shoulders lost their iron grip as King said, "Dean, you look like shit. What the hell's happened to you man?"

Kris lurched forward, putting all of her weight into the movement. She stumbled away from King and didn't give them a second look. Small feet seemed to almost pound the thinly carpeted floor as Kris made her escape.

Kris looked at the four bodies lying before her, blue shrouds stained with various fluids covering their still forms. The gurneys were stainless steel, but they lacked restraints and the hospital wasn't going to use one of the beds with restraints on it to hold down the dead. She shook herself from her revere as she looked at the reinforced walls of the room. There were lockers made to house corpses all around the walls.

There was one door in and out of the room, lessening the chances for the dead to escape if anything happened. It was locked from the outside, and if she needed out the general practice was to go to the camera hung in one of the corners of the room and give the thumbs down sign. However the cameras in the room retrained her from using her precious axe to making sure that the bodies didn't wake up at all. So, all she could do was wait for a few hours until they woke up. The unwritten law as to keep corpses for thirteen hours if the cause of death was something Z-Plague related and on the tenth hour a Watcher could be called in if needed.

So she had three hours to kill keeping an eye on a couple of meat bags that had gotten them killed. She knew on a regular basis that if someone bitten by a zombie and they didn't die instantly they turned within twelve hours, the virus' incubation period. If a person had exchanged fluids with a Z-Plague carrier they had about twenty four hours before they turned because the virus was weaker in those instances.

Sighing she sat down on the floor, laying the axe at her side. Zombies were slow; the old movies had that right. Zombies were dead; their muscles were deteriorating so there wasn't any way that they could run marathons to eat people. In the first few hours they could be sort of fast, but they lacked the brain function and coordination to be too overwhelming.

Kris dug her hand into her jacket pocket and pulled out her iPod and ear buds. She slid the auditory devices into place and began to use the scroll to find something that would keep her totally drowning into boredom. Within moments the heavy guitar licks and melodic vocals of Iron Maiden filled her ears. Her mind began to shift as Irish metal crooned to her, the answer to Ryan the Cute Medical Student's question ringing through her ears.

"Well, you wise up really quickly when your whole class becomes card carrying members of the undead."

She looked over at her axe and her hand went idly for it. The feel of soft leather wrapped over hard steel was as comforting as always against her palm as she picked it up. Scowling, she inspected the blade only to reach into her jeans' pocket and pulled out a whetstone. Within moments the soothing scrape of stone against steel was reverberating through her arms as the song changed segueing from Irish metal to fast punk. The song sent her back into her memories once again.

Juggling her bounty of high fructose corn syrup sweetened soda, processed cheese products, and pastries that could survive a nuclear holocaust, Kris made her way to her one haven. After the ordeal with the Angry Mob she wasn't in the mood to deal with anyone even close to her age group. So she raided the snack machines for things she really shouldn't be eating but couldn't stay away from. Then she took her vastly unhealthy food to the one place the Angry Mob wouldn't be caught dead in: the library.

Kris was greeted by a pair of ordinary brown eyes looked at her from tortoiseshell rimmed glasses set in a face that had seen the tanning bed too many times. Fingers tipped with nails painted a wet, gleaming crimson strummed a shirt with a floral print that even the most ancient of grandmothers would veer away from. "That's not food," came the oddly high-pitched voice from the squat, matronly body.

Kris grinned and replied, "It passes for food, Mrs. Collins."

"You know that stuff's unhealthy. You need to take care of yourself, Kristen, or you're going to be heading for an early grave," Mrs. Collins said with a sigh and a shake of her head.

"Oooh, normally that sort of morbid train of thought is only reserved for me," Kris said as she wiggled her fingers awkwardly at the librarian.

Mrs. Collins sighed and said, "I take it Stephan Skipp and his cronies came at you again, or was it Nichole Lovett and her crew."

"It was the Angry Mob, not the Bevy of Bitches," the teenage girl replied as she placed her bounty down and slid her backpack off of her aching shoulders on the nearest table. She rolled her arms in slow circles before rolling her head in an arch to stretch the tenseness

of carrying a thirty pound back pack on her back. A blast of heavily chilled air rumbled loudly from the air ducts and Kris tilted her head back to take a deep breath of it. Automatically the chilled air started to soothe the firing alveoli in her lungs and a smile stretched across her face.

Mrs. Collins sighed and said, "It is the will of the mass to attack things they don't understand."

"Or who are short, fat and asthmatic and would rather shove their nose in a book than play sports or get pregnant by the age of seventeen. Or who thinks fashion is a huge waste of money and that my Wal-Mart specials are damned comfortable and I don't give a fuck what they think?" Kris asked as she sat down. Within moments the soda can was open with a loud snap and the cheese covered corn chips had already been ripped into. While she was soothing herself with carbonated, caffeine enriched syrup water, Mrs. Collins walked into her office and returned with a heavy hard cover book.

"Well, maybe this will improve your day. If you're going to rot your body, at least your mind's going to stay sharp," Mrs. Collins said with a shake of her head.

Kris' eyes widened at the gorgeous medieval style painting on the cover and began to flip through it. On first inspection the book covered all sorts of aspects from the Crusades and had a large section on the Knight Templers and what they had become. Whistling softly she began to devour the knowledge before her.

Another thing that set her apart from the idiotic mass was her fascination with the past. Anything from the Dark Ages got her immediate attention and anything after World War II seemed to lose her interest. Things on the page, be it fiction or not, captured her attention more than anything the real world had to offer her. As she read, she heard someone else enter the giant library.

She heard Mrs. Collins greet the intruder to her Fortress of Solitude and scowl. There was some shuffling and then she heard a Mrs. Collins scream. Her eyes widened at the spray of blood that came from Mrs. Collins side. The chair fell to the ground as Kris stood from it.

The plump, matronly woman's eyes were so wide that they were showing whites all around them, her arms swinging wildly against her assailant. A crimson stain spread across the horrid print of the librarian's dress as sickly pale fingers dug into her arms. Kris' eyes widened at the filmy grey eyes that focused on her as Mrs. Collins moaned before stop twitching all together.

Fleshy tearing sounds filled the quiet library as the head lifted, exposing bloodied teeth filled with the meat of Mrs. Collins throat. The librarian's body unceremoniously hit the floor as Kris stared at an underclassman who was a member of the basketball team, if her memory of the photos she had logged for the yearbook was any indication. The jock fumbled forward before awkwardly and sluggishly bending over the twitching woman. That bloodied mouth and nearly skeletal hands touched her body and a loud ripping sound accompanied by the loud sounds of chewing filled the room.

"No!" Kris screamed as she grabbed her backpack and charged at the little fucker. Hips pivoted, and surprisingly strong upper body strength caused the heavy bag to swing hard right into the side of the kid's head. A soft moan escaped his lips and he pitched to the side before staggering back on his feet.

"Fucker!" she screeched as she swung again and again. Each heavy blow caused the boy to stagger back, and on the third she heard something crack. However each time she knocked him back he staggered towards her again, his arms lazily outstretched. She looked over at Mrs. Collins, who had stopped moving, her eyes rolled back in her head.

She shouted, "Mrs. Collins! Can you hear me?"

Unsurprisingly there was no answer, no twitch of movement, nothing but stillness. Kris bellowed out as her chest tightened. Gripping the backpack with both hands and twisting to the side ever so slightly, she thrust all her weight forward. Books and short, squat asthmatic teenager hit dead on. Her chest tightened and she was barely aware of the loud, hacking coughs shaking her body as she went down with the thing. She scuttled back as the former basketball player-cum-cannibal attacker floundered on the floor.

The backpack was lifted high and then slammed down again and again. Within moments the black vinyl was wet and dripping with crimson rivulets. Each time the heavy bag made its descent a wet, crunching sound filled the room until there was only a bloody paste smeared on the carpet from where the cannibal's head was.

Hot tears ran down her face as Kris coughed loudly, her chest lurching with each motion and her throat burning. She could feel it swell shut and with shaking hands she grabbed the accursed inhaler from her pocket. With a flick of her thumb the protective cap fell to the ground and with a jerk of her wrist it was shook. The inhaler's mouth piece was warm against her lips as she pressed down to release its contents.

A cold hiss filled the room as the chilled gas filled her throat and then her chest. Lungs expanded and a jolt of energy filled her before her air passages went into spasms to clear what was blocking them. She leaned over to the closest trashcan to clear her throat as large globs of phlegm ejected from her mouth into the trashcan. With shaking hands she shoved her hair from her face as the medicine took effect, fine tremors running through all of her muscles until her hands were practically vibrating. Swallowing, she crawled over to Mrs. Collins' prone form.

The sweet coppery smell that she knew all too well filled her nostrils as she saw the giant crater missing from the librarian's throat. Her skin had taken on an ashy grey tone and those once kind eyes were closed. Kris brought her shaking hands up over Mrs. Collins' heart and began to push. She counted five compressions before tilting the woman's head back, holding her nose closed and breathing into her mouth. She repeated the process over and over again, tiny sobs escaping her throat each time she felt something crack under her hands.

There was no flutter of a heart beat under her hands, no movement of air and only an increasing stillness coming from Mrs. Collins. Kris was sobbing, tears obscuring her vision as she worked on the next round of compressions. She was screaming at the woman, not words, just loud demanding cries that made no sense as she moved. At the fifth compression Kris moved to breathe into her mouth again when Mrs. Collins' sat up with a retching moan.

Filmy eyes looked over at Kris as the bloodied librarian lunged at her. Kris cried out and scrambled away, but Mrs. Collins was on her, snapping her teeth violently as she tried to get at Kris' throat. Kris held up her hands with a scream as she pushed the *woman's snapping jaws back. Teeth sank into soft flesh and pain shot up her wrist, her arm and through her body in a sharp rush that caused her to scream. She kicked up with all of her might, throwing the woman back.*

Scrambling to her feet, Kris fled her personal sanctuary only to enter an all new circle of hell.

Kris flexed her left hand and looked at the faint scar that still adorned it, a reminder of the day that had changed her life forever. Short fingers extended to reveal the near perfect indentations of human teeth and the forever proof that showed her immunity to the Z-Plague. After fleeing the library she had found that most of her school had turned into zombies too.

Apparently killing former tormenters who had turned into the undead and were trying to eat you was the best sort of therapy she'd ever had. She wasn't sure what had happened, but she knew enough on how to survive. Luckily the workshop had been close enough to the library where she had grabbed a fire axe. Ironically, King was the second zombie she had killed and to this day she could still see the pus pouring down his face from his blemishes after death.

After she had managed to escape the high school of the dead she had been taken to the local hospital. Massive amounts of blood tests were run, and apparently she was immune to the Z-Plague to the fact she wasn't even a carrier. Some of the doctors she would later meet wondered if it was her accursed inhaler or condition that kept her from getting the virus. She wasn't sure and she wasn't going to start wondering now.

At the time Kris figured she'd finish high school and then go onto college to get a degree that would be almost useless to anyone who wasn't a teacher, which would have been fine with her. However the US government had different ideas and a lot of money to offer her if she joined them. Money enough to spend most of her days in a book when she wasn't working, but she had to be on call to kill zombies and on occasions give blood for testing. First she started helping with outbreaks, and then she had been promoted as a Watcher of the Dead to make sure that people didn't come back as zombies, and if she did she'd give them eternal rest.

Hell, she even had a professional blacksmith make her the trademark axe she always carried and she always made sure to keep it sharp.

Pay the executioner to keep her blade sharp, she thought with a chuckle as she looked at her watch. She sighed and said aloud, "One more fucking hour to go. Thank God. You know, I need to bring a book or something when I do this, or people are going to think I'm fucking nutters. Well, I am talking to myself."

She got up and started to pace, nodding at the cameras in the room as she approached them. The iPod had been turned off to conserve its battery and it wasn't going to be turned on again until some corpses were moving. "Kris, I've got movement on the left," Ryan's voice said over the intercom.

"Showtime," she said with a smirk as she turned to the shrouded figure on the left. The legs and feet were twitching, and a moment later it sat straight up. The stained blue shroud fell forward, revealing molted grey and bruised skin, filmy eyes and an open, moaning mouth. Arms outstretched towards her as it began to shift from its perch. With a grin she reached for her iPod and switched it on.

Pounding punk music and nonsensical lyrics poured through her ears as the axe swung up. The weight felt good and the momentum drove the blade straight into the center of the zombie's head. With a jerk blood squirted out in a near black arch as she spun to the remaining three corpses that were starting to stir and sit up as well. With a smirk and a loud cry, she charged them as well.

"Holy shit," Ryan said aloud as he watched the black and white image on the screen before him. Bruce had taken another smoke break and Joyce had gone home before the second hour, so he was alone to watch the carnage on the screen before him. For the past two hours he'd been watching the Watcher and the dead. He felt like some perverse voyeur as Kris Campbell had become obviously lost in her thoughts as he wondered what was going on through her mind as she sat alone with four dead people.

Then the bodies had started to rise. He had gotten on the com to warn her because she was pacing around the room like a caged animal. Ryan had expected her to calmly stand in front of the bodies, raise the axe up and bring it down. The primal display of the small girl swinging the axe while letting out a battle cry with a grin wasn't what he'd expected. Yet he felt his body starting to stand at attention as she made steel cleave flesh and blood spray as she gave the dead their final rights.

Within moments later she was giving the thumbs up to the camera and he scrambled from his seat. Swallowing hard, he cursed his short lab coat as he tried to arrange it so she wouldn't see his reaction to watching her at work. He ran to the heavy steel door and opened it. Kris' apple green eyes were sparkling and there was a red streak across one cheek as she smiled at him.

He whistled and said, "That was . . ."

"Wasn't what you expected?" she asked with a smirk as she shouldered her gore splattered axe.

Ryan cleared his throat and said, "Well, yeah, but . . . it was *awesome*."

Kris blinked and a pretty flush stained her rounded

cheeks as she stammered, "Really?"

"Yeah, so . . . what do you think of coffee?" he asked as he gave her a hopeful look.

She blinked as the blush grew darker and asked, "Are you asking me on a date?"

"That would have been the purpose of my inquiry," he said with a lopsided grin as he rubbed the back of his head.

A delightful laugh bubbled from her lips before she said, "Okay . . . And here I thought I was crazy . . . I mean, Watchers of the Dead don't exactly lead normal lives."

"Well, they should have a life," Ryan said as he grabbed a pen and paper. His hands worked rapidly as he left his cell phone number and email address. For extra measure he even put on his Facebook information and passed it to her. "It's only if you want to," he added with a shrug.

Those fingers with their gunmetal painted nails deftly folded the sheet of paper and tucked it into one of the jacket's many pockets. She flashed him a grin and said, "Well, this is an unusual turn of events for me. Guys generally aren't knocking down my door to ask me out."

"Their loss is my gain," Ryan said with a smile, "Hey, just because zombies are wandering around doesn't mean that life doesn't go on."

Kris' smile broadened even more at that and she said, "Yeah, you're right. Just because I Watch the fucking dead doesn't mean I can't live right?"

"Right," Ryan said as he handed her a piece of paper and the pin, "So, why don't you give me those digits and we can try living."

Her eyes never leaving his face she began to write on the paper and said, "I'd like that."

UNDERTAKER'S CHAINS
BY JIM BRONYAUR

They think I dress in black because it's part of the job. They think I'm some giant looming figure who walks slowly in between graves, keeping the dead at peace. They even call me by the wrong name most of the time too. They call me an undertaker, which bothers some caretakers or funeral directors, but for me, I prefer undertaker. Because it does sound a lot tougher and somber.

My job isn't necessarily to bury people, but rather prepare them and their families for the once in a lifetime moment (yes, pun intended). I don't hover over the empty grave and shovel in dirt with thick black gloves on my hands or with black sweat pouring out of me. I don't gently tap the fresh mound of dirt once the grave is full.

Believe it or not, there are people that I pay to do those things. My job is stand in the background, normally in my best suit (the only Amy bought for me three years ago when I took over the family business). I wait until everyone is gone and then say my final words to the family members. I also hand out my card and offer to talk any time. Not because I'm some sleaze salesman, but because I enjoy talking to people.

Why?

Because most mornings, afternoons, and early evenings, until the news and game shows start, I spend with the dead.

I get to prepare their bodies for burial. Yes, all the gross stuff you've heard about – draining their blood and fluids. Putting new fluids in. Cleaning them up. Dressing them. All that fun stuff.

And I do it in the basement of a windowless room that's got off-colored white tile because my father refused to put a dime into the basement. He kept the upstairs looking nice for "customers" and the rest went into his pocket.

But that's a whole other story.

This story is about Thursday, April 29, 2010 – the day the dead came alive.

Three bodies came in the day before. Mr. Barrington, a man who worked at the local steel plant for thirty years until they shut it down. He then took an early retirement and used his savings to open a little hardware store. He passed it down to his kids who promptly closed it, turned it into a bar, and is now renamed The Hardware Bar. It makes more money than a hardware store ever would, but I could always tell Mr. Barrington wished it stayed a hardware store. He was 87. Death due to natural causes.

The second was Miss Cress. She was, get this, three weeks shy of her one hundredth birthday. She was also a witch. Well, not a real witch, but she was the one who refused to give out Halloween candy and would chase kids off her sidewalks with a broom. Death due to massive heart attack. I still don't understand how a heart that old can have a massive heart attack, but hey, I don't write the reports.

Finally, there was a 47 year old man, Jerry Carver. That one bothered me. I'm other than Jerry and it didn't feel right preparing a body that was younger than me.

I saved Jerry for last.

Now, the entire time I prepared Mr. Barrington and Miss Cress, everything was fine. The bodies cooperated and they were done in no time. I say cooperate because sometimes they get hit with rigor mortis so soon and so bad it's like trying to straighten out a bent, rotted log.

With those two done, I forced myself to eat an early lunch. I was avoiding Jerry the best I could. My job does have it tough parts; including the questioning of why people die the way they do, when they do.

Once my lunch was gone, I really had no choice; I had to tend to Jerry. His viewing was a day away and I still had to meet with his brother Jacob (or was it Jamie… oh well, I had notes upstairs) to discuss some final options. But until that time came, I had a job to do. He may have been only 47, but Jerry was dead. And being dead required me to drain his fluids and preserve his body.

See, I probably approach embalming a body the way an athlete prepares for a big game or a musician prepares for the big show. I stand in the back hallway of the basement, taking heavy breaths. I visualize myself draining the blood. I visualize not spilling a drop. I visualize the finished product. Then I charge down the hallway, letting my coat open and sometimes (oh boy, I hate admitting this part), but sometimes I actually close my eyes and put my hands out touching the rough cement walls and pretend I'm slapping hands with diehard fans.

Then I'm there, with the body, ready to go.

Tools in place.

My heart racing.

Gloves on.

Fresh coat on.

No sound.

No music.

Make cut, insert tubing.

Drain blood.

Sweating now…

It's such an amazing process.

I was "in the zone" as some people call it. I was so focused that all the lights could have gone out and I probably could have finished the process.

Then, like I mentioned earlier, all hell broke loose.

Jerry threw his right arm in the air.

That broke my concentration and I jumped back. I pulled the tube out of his neck and blood started to squirt everywhere. It all happened so quick, I wasn't sure if I imagined Jerry moving or not.

The tube lay on the floor, pushing blood out like it was its own pulsating vein.

"Jerry?" I whispered. "Are you… alive?"

Then a hand grabbed my shoulder.

It was a bony hand.

I turned around and Mr. Barrington was sitting up, smiling at me. He tried to open his mouth but couldn't. See, we sew their mouths shut so there aren't any scary scenes during the viewing. You know, grandma opening her mouth while grandpa says his goodbye.

"Mr. Barrington?" I asked. I reached out for a quick second and then realized he was done. His blood was gone. He was full of embalming fluid.

I grabbed his hand and pushed it off my shoulder.

I stepped back.

I felt another hand grab me.

I turned again, this time towards the wall so I could have full view of what the hell was going on.

Jerry was sitting up. He stuck his thumb into his neck to stop the bleeding.

"Jerry, are you alive?" I screamed.

Jerry started to chew on his tongue. But there was no way he was alive. They had just done an autopsy on the poor guy. He had a massive "Y" carved from his shoulders down to his groin. It was stitched up with thick, black thread. No way could he be alive again.

But he was.

Then Miss Cress started. She tossed and turned and then sat straight up. She turned her head towards me, blinked once, and then turned her head some more. After a few agonizing cracks, her head spun all the way around. Needless to say, my lunch made its return. Then when the chunks of ham started to mix with the blood, I bent over, dry heaving.

Jerry wiggled himself to the edge of the table and

started to mimic me, only spitting up blood and some kind of greens chunks of whatever. He reached out for me with his free hand and I swatted it away.

Mr. Barrington put his long, skinny legs to the floor and tried to stand up.

Miss. Cress kept spinning her head round and round.

I was frozen. I can handle a lot of things, trust me, I've seen a lot. But this... this was something they do not teach you in school. There is no chapter or appendix or case study titled *"What to do when they come alive..."*

I started to try and think logically for a second. They were dead. The coroner said so. The autopsy report on Jerry said so. Two were drained and embalmed, the other had its organs cut out like a high school science project.

Jerry kept rocking back and forth and poor Mr. Barrington, he kept acting like the floor was on fire. He would touch the floor and then pull away. Then he would look at me and try to yell.

"Oott," he would call out. "Ss..oott."

"That's okay," I said to him. "Just relax."

Then I heard the sound of things scraping together. Miss Cress was now twisting her wrist round and round. My stomach jumped.

I needed to put an end to this.

Now, my brain may not have been in the right spot at that moment, as you can expect. So I ran out of the room, to the back room. I found a small tool box and took out a hammer.

Why?

I don't know. It seemed right.

I came charging back in and cough a few times, building up what I hoped would be the toughest voice I could come up with.

"Okay, I'm giving you deceased person's one chance to lie back into the positions you belong so I may finish the process."

Wow, did that go over well…

Jerry started to laugh at me so hard he put his hands to his mouth which meant he took his thumb from his neck. Each time he laughed, blood shot out towards Mr. Barrington, soaking him from his kneecaps down.

Mr. Barrington slapped the table in a weird pattern.

Miss Cress hunched over and took her ankle and twisted it.

SNAP.

I lost it.

I couldn't take it anymore.

I walked up to Jerry and smacked him in the head with the hammer. Then he fell back and was gone. Again. Just like that.

I repeated the process with Mr. Barrington and Miss Cress and as quick as it started, it was over.

I had three dead corpses on my tables. Miss Cress's limbs were stringy. But I had an idea of how to fix it. Superglue and sticks. Don't ask.

Mr. Barrington needed a fresh set of stitching in his mouth and the blood cleaned off his legs.

Jerry, 47 year old Jerry, he needed some work.

But I did it. I finished up just in time to hear the lottery numbers being called. That meant one more minute until the game shows started.

I told myself I would fix the dents in their heads in the morning. A little touch up makeup and some fancy lighting would do the trick.

As I left the room that night, I did something I'd never thought I'd do – I took the dog chains my father kept in the storage closet and chained the three bodies down.

I tugged one last time on Jerry and felt comfortable knowing that even if they came alive again, they couldn't move much.

Then a terrible thought occurred to me… growing up, we never had dogs.

CORPSE EATER
BY JONATHAN MOON

Even though he is fairly new to the mortician game, Marty Newstead has a deep and dismal feeling rolling in his gut as he walks up the staircase to the Stillwater Funeral Home. He tells himself it is first day jitters coupled with the fact his chosen profession (as an undertaker) is the personification of macabre to most people. Not to mention he was actually called in a night early due to an emergency in Dry Hill, forty-five minutes down mountain. It is Marty's first night and he's going to be flying solo while the head mortician sees to the emergency out of town.

A series of small ornate lamps light the wide stone steps and the porch light above the door cast long shadows from the potted trees that line the large stone porch. An old stone archway surrounds the door with an ominous gargoyle glaring down at Marty from its apex. The large darkened building looks like the bastard child of a lumber factory and Victorian Mansion, with the basement and rear of the building used for the town's mortuary and morgue and the front being the elegant funeral home complete with a room large enough to handle any funeral for the surrounding area. It is a damn big building for a lot of little towns. It looms over the near-by houses, most of which are decrepit and empty. The long brick chimney even towers over a few of the two hundred year old pines that shade the town. Marty knocks and the face that answers is a sharp contrast to the gloomy aura hanging over the property.

"Hello, Mr. Newstead, thank you so much for helping me out here."

Niles 'Ripper' Jensen, the head mortician, opens the door wide to let Marty in. Having only spoken to Ripper, as he swore his friends called him, over the phone Marty immediately relaxes when he sees the man is only a year or two out of college himself. He isn't an inch over five feet tall but his smile is so big and genuine it actually makes him seem taller. His two inch platform boots helped with that as well. Ripper's dark hair is short and slicked back and his tattooed forearms are vibrant against the stark white of his smock. He notices Marty's gaze.

"I see ya checking out my ink," Ripper says and steps closer as he rolls up his smock sleeve to his shoulder, "I gotta guy in Falterwood that does sick work. Ha! Two morticians talking about 'sick work'!"

He cracks himself up with his joke and Marty can't help but chuckle along.

"I think we'll get along fine," Ripper says with a nod. "Let me give ya the quickee tour so I can bounce down to Dry Hill and stuff that stiff. Hopefully I can be back within the next two hours and help you with the triple header shot gun homicide you got waitin' on ya downstairs!"

The dismal feeling tugs in Marty's gut again. His eyes widen and his nervous smile wanes. Ripper's smile doesn't.

"HA! I'm just fucking with you, new kid. Ya' only got two and neither one is a shot gun. Ya got an old age we gotta cook and a rock climber with a broken fucking neck. Hey, you like Metallica?"

Marty laughs despite his nervousness which remains despite the joke.

"Yeah, I guess."

Ripper leads Marty through a nice hallway decorated with hundreds of photos and a few large wooden framed mirrors. He walks to a curtain covered wall and slides the dark green curtains to the side revealing metal double doors. He turns back to Marty as he opens the door.

"They had a bassist named Jason Newstead after bass god Cliff Burton died in a bus crash. So the rest of the band always called Newstead 'New Kid.' I think after years it finally fucking got to him cuz he fucking bounced. He left

Metallica, one of the biggest fucking metal bands ever! You ain't gonna bounce if I call ya New Kid are ya?"

Ripper's easy nature did it's best to calm Marty's nervous stomach. When Marty laughs it is sincere but still shaky with nervousness.

"Na, I need the money."

"Right on," Ripper grins, "Well, this up here is the funeral home."

He waves a small tattooed arm around the dark room.

"We'll check it out when I'm not in a hurry. It is creepy and old and smells like death, so, if you're like me you'll dig it."

He pushes and the doors open with a squeal that echoes around the two men. He nods towards the staircase, allows Marty past, and as he lets the door shut he tells him, "The party's down here!"

Ripper gives Marty a rushed tour with as many facts about mid-eighties and nineties thrash bands as the simple necessities for taking care of the two bodies tonight. Ripper catches sight of his watch mid-way through the tour and says, "Shit! I gotta get the hell outta here. Hey, listen man, be sure to get old man Vickerson cooking before you start slicing on the clumsy climber, alright? It's an old ass oven and we gotta warm that son of a bitch up, so set a timer. Wait for it and make sure he's cooking before your cutting. Important!"

"Okay." Marty nods.

"All right I'll hurry back; hopefully we can bond over gutting up that broken neck. You got any questions, New Kid?"

"Yeah, a few."

"Well, ask fast."

"I've never seen a funeral home the city owns. Is that common around here?"

"Nope. The place used to be called 'The Baxter Family Funeral Home' but something happened and the town took it over. Next."

"How long have you been working here?"

"About ten months. They have a hell of a time keeping morticians around here. I'll explain later on, just remember cook before cut!"

Ripper smiles, grabs his coat and bounds up the stairs two at a time. Marty hears his foot falls across the ceiling above him and the dismal feeling in his gut stirs in the silence that follows. He convinces himself this is what he signed on for and he sets about his work. He walks into the crematorium and sets the faded old knob timer on the ancient furnace. Marty has been in crematoriums before and none have ever reeked like this one. A strong strange chemical smell lingers alongside the typical burnt death smell of such old ovens. Marty shivers but thinks of how nice a paycheck will be. He shuts the door to the crematorium and thinks of how nice it will be to pay some of the school loans he's got off. How good it will feel to show his dad that he can make money at his chosen trade.

Marty takes a small walk through the rooms he had been rushed through moments before. He makes mental notes of where what tools are kept. He makes a mental map of the basement and as he lays out the tools he'll need for the climber he hums a funeral dirge. Marty pulls both men out of their cold drawers; placing the climber on the steel table and Mr. Vickerson on a steel gurney so he can wheel him into the oven. He looks at his watch and tells the old man's corpse, "That should be long enough to cook your skinny ass, old fella."

He pushes the gurney down the small fluorescent lit hallway still whistling his dark melody. His slams the gurney into the door and it swings open with a clatter. Marty gags as he follows the gurney into the room. The chemical smell burns his eyes and throat but he can see the door to the cremator is wide open through his sudden tears. Black slime drips boiling down the side and pools at its base. Clumps of ash litter the floor and stick to the chemical-reeking slime. Marty covers his mouth and nose and squints through watery eyes at the temperature gauge. He moans in frustration when he sees it isn't near as hot as it needs to be to reduce old man Vickerson to little gray ash balls yet. Marty slams the door to the cremator shut and double checks the timer. He pushes the gurney holding Vickerson to the side of the room and decides to get a start on cutting up the climber.

The chemical smell hits Marty like a poke in the eye when he opens the door to the hallway. A strange dragging trail of the black ash covered slime leads down the hallway towards the room with the dead climber in it. The steel door swings lightly, waving the chemical odor back down the hall at Marty. He freezes one step outside the door to the crematorium and pulls his cell phone from his apron. He dials Ripper's cell phone and takes a slow step forward.

Wet tearing sounds echo from the room ahead. The phone rings and Marty takes another step.

A monstrous snarl then a second more intense tearing sound echo ahead. The phone rings again and Marty wagers two more steps.

Gulping sounds twist Marty's stomach but his natural and morbid curiosity has him taking steps even as the phone rings again.

Ripper answers his phone and all Marty can hear at first are a few lines from Testament's 'Return to Serenity'. The volume decreases just as the line disintegrates to static. The sick feeling prompts Marty to take a few steps back from the door ahead and whisper into the phone.

"Uh, Mr. Jensen, err, Ripper, this is Marty."

Static crackles the connection and Ripper shouts into Marty's ear.

"New Kid! Hey, I'm on my way back. The line is breaking up something fierce, everything 'ite?"

Marty tries to tell him something is wrong with the crematorium but the line buzzes and crackles before dying. Marty curses while closing his phone. More disgusting sounds are echoing out of the cadaver room; snarls, slurps, chewing, and tearing sounds.

The sick feeling rolls and clenches Marty's stomach but he is walking back towards the door his stubborn mind sharp against his weak stomach.

A prank. He thinks to himself. *That Ripper dude is hazing me.*

Marty reaches the door and places one hand inches from the door.

Just get this over with. No gory little prank is going to scare you away from this job. Tighten that tummy up and show this little prick you don't spook at the sight of a little gore.

Marty takes one last breath in a feeble attempt to calm his twisting gut before he pushes the door wide open. The chemical reek is stronger than it was in the crematorium or the hallway and it makes Marty swoon and his eyes blur. He covers his mouth and nose with one hand and wipes the tears from his weeping eyes with his other.

Perched on top of the steel table with the climber's corpse is a humanoid creature with both its arms hidden in the dead body's chest cavity. Its face is half black and half pink, with small bristles poking out over all the blackened flesh. The jaw hangs wide open (three times as wide as any human could open their mouth), is lined with tiny sharp teeth, and dribbles chemical slime onto the body below it where it sizzles the cold dead flesh. The creature's rail thin body is covered in the same black bristly skin where there aren't patches of white fabric burnt to the flesh. The thing has long slender legs tucked under it and its long spindly arms flex as they dig in the corpse. Marty notices that the corpse's legs are chewed and mangled stumps at both knees. The feeling in his stomach is turning into something sour creeping up his throat.

The thing turns its glowing orange eyes on Marty. Marty backs into the door way, smacking his head on the steel. The creature opens its mouth impossibly wide and screeches at Marty; spraying him with chunks of cold gore.

The thing pulls two handfuls of gray and pink organs from the cadaver's chest and gorges on them with brutal chewing and slurping sounds. Marty screams like he has never screamed before. The creature responds by hurling a handful of mashed dead guts at the screaming man. The ground-up organs hit Marty in his chest. His stomach, solid steel through all of his schooling, heaves and Marty vomits his dinner down his gore-soaked smock. The thing stands on the table but has to duck from hitting the low ceiling above. It reaches a clawed hand back into the chest for more goodies. As it pulls at the corpse's innards the cadaver jerks and tears. The beast stuffs the last handful of cold guts into his mouth and dives at Marty. Marty sees the thing leap towards him but it moves too fast for him to run away. He raises his arms to cover his face, he smells the chemical reek, and his knees go weak. The monster slams through the door next to Marty and, relieved, Marty lets the darkness take him.

The first thing Marty hears when he starts to come to is Exodus' 'Bonded by Blood' blaring from the small beat-up CD player Ripper keeps next to his work table. Marty opens his eyes slowly and silently scans the room. Ripper is singing along to the classic thrash album with his back to Marty while he works on the climber's dead body. Marty leans up, feels the wet throb on the back of his head, notices his gore and vomit covered smock, and groans.

Ripper turns around with an impish grin.

"Good morning, new kid. Some crazy shits go down? Or are you just a shitty mortician?"

"No," Marty says while rubbing the goose egg on his head. The memory of the corpse eating monster is vivid and surreal and he tells Ripper, "Something was eating him. Holy shit, it was the most fucked up thing I've ever seen."

"And it scared you so bad you passed out?"

"Well, yeah, I thought it was gonna eat me."

"Nah, you ain't dead. It ate half of Vickerson before I scared it back into the oven when I got back. Shit, new kid, I already had to catch a coupla' alley cats to fill up his urn. Damn lucky this town is swarming with strays, huh?"

"You knew about that *thing*?"

"Yeah, I shoulda' told you about all this." Ripper looks at the half devoured corpse on the table and takes off his latex gloves and tosses them into the trash. He sits on the floor next to Marty.

"That was old man Baxter. Like, the funeral home used to be named after."

"Is this a sick joke? Because I don't think it's funny." Now that terror is passing anger is replacing it in Marty's shocked mind.

"Nope. No joke. Let me tell you a quick little story, 'ite?"

Unable to tell if he is being had or not, Marty just says, "Fine."

Ripper stands up and offers Marty a hand; which he takes. Marty sways on weak knees and notices Ripper has re-sewn the corpse closed and even dressed it in its burial clothes. The legless pants hang limply off the side of the table. The chemical smell still lingers lightly in the air but Ripper has mopped up the ash and slime.

"So, about sixty years ago Chuck Baxter ran this place. His great granddaddy opened it and ran it for years. The building and the profession where passed down through the Baxter family until old Chuck, there. Well, somewhere along the line Chuck's brain warped and he decided he enjoyed the taste of dead meat. No one knows how long he had been cutting off pieces of the bodies he worked on but one hot summer day the whole town found out."

"How?'

"Well, they were burying a sweet little girl named Cindy Maskiss and after the viewing but before the actual burial her momma snuck in and lifted the coffin lid to give her baby girl one last goodbye. Instead she saw the corpse of her daughter with stumps where her legs should have been. Her reaction was immediate and severe. As was that of the funeral party. The people, already grief-stricken and distraught, attacked the morbid mortician and dragged him down here. Men, women, and children beat him with fists, feet, and table legs. They drug him to the embalming room and held him down while they stuck tubes down his throat, up his ass, and in his ears. The entire funeral party stood and howled while they pumped the still living Baxter full of deadly chemicals."

"Damn."

"Yeah, damn, but they still weren't done yet. They carried his twitching smoking body to the crematorium and tossed him into the oven alive. They laughed and hugged as the villain screamed in ungodly agony right there next to them all. The story goes he was still screaming and moaning at intervals when the place emptied out. The city took over the property and it became one of those things the people never talk about. All that wasn't enough though, cuz the creepy old bastard still sneaks out of the crematorium for mid-night snacks every now and then. That's why no one wants to work here. I can't say I blame them, watching him eat is just fucking nasty, and I'm a morbid dude. I cleaned it all up this time but now that you are working here too, I ain't cleaning up after his crazy ass all the time. You hear me? You got next, new kid."

"Yeah."

"So you're staying on?"

"Yeah, I need the cash."

The two share an awkward smile at their dark secret. Marty sighs and asks, "So what do we do now?"

Ripper stands up adjusts the tie on the legless corpse and tells Marty, "Now, we just pray no one checks to make sure this guy is wearing his favorite climbing shoes."

UNDERTAKERS DON'T MAKE HOUSE CALLS:
A TALE OF MORTIMER CAINE
BY MIKE MITCHELL

Mortimer Caine never understood why the stovepipe hat went out of style. Undertakers these days had no sense of style. Nice black suit, a tie and that was it. Gone was the day when the undertaker commanded respect in the community. Now they were just a sad side note in the life cycle, someone no one wanted to see but everyone would, come their time. The Nether Realm, however, respected the Undertakers. In that dimension, the undertaker commanded authority over those souls and beings that wanted to visit the Light Side, the world of the living. The Undertakers were the caretakers of the boundaries between the living and the dead, and anyone who wanted to enter the other side had to go through them. They were a bit like border patrols, only with more demons and zombies, an afterlife police force, regulating the flow of the supernatural into the living realm. These passages tended to gather near funeral homes or areas of great tragedy, the energies of the dead being so prominent in these places.

Tonight, however, was a slow night. In his 150 years on this earth, doing this job, Mortimer learned to enjoy the slow nights. No goblins knocking at his door asking for passes to Amsterdam, no Kacko-Demons looking for hunting permits, however there was one drunken vampire that stopped by looking for a pack of smokes. Mortimer pointed him to the convenience store up the road.

Mortimer's living space, above his funeral home, was lavishly decorated. Set in early Victorian décor, deep reds with eccentric patterns on the furniture and wall hangings, the shelves were full of mystical objects, charms and talismans. Human skulls that could summon fire elementals, the ground hooves of this, the severed hand of that with a little bit of eye of something else thrown in for good measure. It wasn't often that Mortimer had to go into battle, but it was known throughout the Nether Realm that Mortimer Caine was not someone to fuck with if you wanted to keep your afterlife. Even though he was skinny and over 100 years old, Mortimer still looked to be in his 20's, the same age when he was called up by Keepers Council, and very tone, his loose fitting clothing hiding the lithe muscles underneath. Nether Siders where technically dead, but that didn't mean they couldn't die, and where they went after that, well, no one was quite too sure.

Mortimer walked to his refrigerator and pulled out a beer and cracked the top open. Foam welled up from the opening and spilled over his hand. Mortimer sucked up the foam, placed the beer on the counter grabbed a cloth and began to clean his hands and the floor.

Mortimer was on his knees wiping up the puddle of foam when the lights flickered and dimmed. An image of a shadowy bat suddenly appeared on the opposite wall. Mortimer looked up at the candle that cast the reflection, its glass covering he had blackened himself leaving clear just the shape of a bat for the light to shine through. What could he say, he loved the comic books. Mortimer sighed and stood. Whatever had lit the candle was entreating an audience with him.

He walked over to the large dish that sat beside the candle and grabbed a handful of powder. Closing his eyes Mortimer began to whisper, grounding his energies to the floor, feeling the power of the portal between realms fill him, flowing from his feet up to his head. "May the lines be drawn and the borders thin, let the audience be met, by my will, come forth!" He blew the dust from his hand onto the candle, which burst into blue flame in midair. A patch of floor lit up, a circle, until needed, unseen, drawn on the hard wood with strange symbols ringing the edges. A light burst forth from the circle and a small red demon, sharp teeth and cloven feet appeared in the center. It was dressed in a double-breasted suit and tie, luminescent blue and black. It flexed its claws in the air and growled.

"Jesus Cyrus, if you hate traveling by magic you could always try the front door. Beer?" Mortimer asked and walked back towards the kitchen.

"Morty, you old flesh bag! Hell yes I want a beer!" the small demon replied in a sort of New York accent. Reaching into his coat, he pulled out a cigar and placed it in his lips, looking comically oversized considering his small stature. Flicking his fingers, a small flame shot out of his thumb as he placed the tip of the cigar to it, he puffed deeply, enjoying the flavor. Mortimer returned and handed Cyrus a beer and flopped down in his easy chair, motioning for Cyrus to sit on the couch.

"Is this a social call or are you here on business, Cy? You know, cuz if you want, I could kick your ass on the PlayStation again." Cyrus was Mortimer's contact on the Dead Side and his good friend. Sort of a secretary, Cyrus handled the scheduling and appointments for audiences from that side. Cyrus only popped up like this when something was going down or he needed a sound thrashing on the PlayStation.

"Business Morty, sorry to say. We got reports in the Nether about a 4-16 down on Wabash. Getting pretty rough I hear, people evacuating the house."

"Damnit, Cy. You know I hate Poltergeists." A 4-16 was a poltergeist haunting with human injuries. Violence against the Live Siders was strictly prohibited by the Shadow Treaty and punishable by banishment to the Dead Side with all Live Side privileges revoked for a couple hundred years, or until the council says otherwise. Poltergeists could be the most childish of all Dead Siders, and they never wanted to come peacefully.

Mortimer walked to the shelf and grabbed an amulet sliding it over his neck, snatched up a ring that was placed on his left pinky finger and shoved a talisman that looked like a bird into his coat pocket.

Cyrus was busy pulling out a map and dagger and placed them on the table. Cyrus found the house on the map and plunged the dagger into the location of the disturbance. The knife thudded deeply as it sunk home into the map and the table.

"God damnit Cy," Mortimer said, "that's my table."

"You know, if you kept an alter like any magic user worth his weight, I wouldn't have to put holes in your furniture." Cyrus said, dismissively, taking a deep puff of his cigar.

"Ya well, that shit looks tacky, and you know me, the paragon of fashion." Mortimer said, throwing on his trench coat and fedora.

"Ya, because looking like a reject from a Mickey Spillane novel is in this season. Just get going, will 'ya?"

"The dagger set?"

"Just waiting for your word. And, Morty… you really need better beer," Cy said, picking up his beer and taking a drink.

"Ha frickin ha. Don't drink it then, Cy." Mortimer saluted with a middle finger, closed his eyes and concentrated on the dagger in the map, showing him the location of the 4-16. A mumbled Latin phrase and a sensation of being squeezed through a lemon zester later, and Mortimer was standing outside of the house on Wabash Avenue.

Lights blinked on and off, the sounds of crashing furniture and the occasional scream of a disembodied voice pierced the otherwise quiet night. Poltergeists.

Mortimer stepped up to the door and tried the handle. It turned and he pushed the door open and started to step inside when the door suddenly jerked back closed in his face. Mortimer sighed and braced himself. "By the authority vested in me by The Keepers Council and The Shadow Treaty, I demand that you stand down any haunting activities and grant me passage inside. It's cold out here, kiddies, and it is not improving my mood." He said in his most commanding voice. The lights and sounds stopped dead and all was silent for a moment before the door clicked and creaked open a crack. Mortimer pushed the door open and stepped in as the door slammed shut again behind him. Mortimer looked around at the chaos surrounding him. The furniture overturned, books and drawers littered the floors, and the back wall was charred from some kind of fire.

"GET OUT!" rang a deep voice, coming from nowhere, yet everywhere at once.

"Look, I'm an Undertaker, here by the authority of the Keepers Council…"

"GET OUT!" came a higher voice from the television and the stereo speakers.

"I'm here to take you…" Mortimer started again but was cutoff.

"Do you see?" asked the deeper voice. "He can't even come up with his own ideas. What happened to the classics? Blood flowing from the walls. A horde of flies against the windows. The young these days…" and the voiced harrumphed.

"Uhm… excuse me?" Mortimer asked.

"It's not my fault you older ones can't get with the picture these days. It's a new era and you need new tricks old man," replied the higher voice.

"I've been haunting since before you were a Live One, I think I know how to do my job," replied the deeper voice, agitated.

"Excuse me…" Mortimer said again, getting irritated.

"People today aren't scared as easy as they were in your day, it takes something more than just special effects to get into these flesh bags heads" The higher voice said back and rumbled the house.

"EXCUSE ME!" Mortimer yelled and raised his hand in the air, pushing his energies into the ring on his finger, causing a bright light to explode from it, getting the attention of the spooks.

"WHAT?" the voices yelled in unison.

"Now that I have your attention, my name is Mortimer Caine, Undertaker. I'm here on authority of the Keepers Council to bring you to the Nether Realm to stand in response to injuries inflicted on the Live Ones."

"Oh that," said the deeper voice. "I tried telling him to get out and find his own haunting, but no. I was happy to make the walls bleed and float the occasional baby, but no! This 'child' just had to go and throw things around, had to show how big his protoplasm is and upstage me. I told him, I said, you're gonna piss off the council, but would he listen? NO! And now look who's here. I hope you're happy."

"Gramps, it's a new era, and I'm not going to bow down before some council. If they can't handle the way things are done now-a-days, that's not my problem. It's time for your generation to step aside and let us show you how things are done."

"That's enough! Both of you!" Mortimer shouted. "Your both coming with me to the Nether Realm and the council can figure out what happens next."

"I'm not going anywhere flesh bag!" The younger geist shouted and flung Mortimer across the room, crashing into the wall. Mortimer slid down and landed in a heap on the floor, groaning.

"This isn't going to end well," the older geist said.

"Shut it old man," the younger one replied.

Mortimer stood and groaned, rubbing his neck. "Look kid, we can do this the easy way or the fun way. If you wanna dance, I'll dance, but you ain't gonna like the song." Books and furniture lifted into the air around him and the fireplace burst into flames, a column shooting out towards Mortimer like a finger trying to poke him in the ribs.

Mortimer gathered up his will and focused on the ring, a shield of bright light appeared in front of him, scattering the flame. He reached into his pocket as the heat threatened to sear his face and pulled out the talisman. Mortimer gathered up his energies and pushed once again through the ring, expanding the shield forward, pushing the flame back and rolled himself away, out of the path of the fireplace.

Mortimer slammed the talisman on the ground 3 times and yelled "By the will of Amon'kay, I demand you reveal your form!" The air rippled outwards in a bubble, enveloping everything in it. The furniture dropped to the floor and the fire died out and two forms, visible but translucent, appeared before him. The first was dressed like a man from the 1800's. Hat, boots, vest, gun belt, the works. The second wore what would have been leather pants, if it had physical form, a Mohawk and piercings with a Ramones T-shirt. The younger geist threw its hand wildly in the air, trying to fling Mortimer again, but nothing happened. It looked at his arm and flung again, but Mortimer stayed in place.

"Told you," Mortimer said. "Now, we can do this respectfully. Name, haunting permit, ID number and date of death, if you please."

The younger geist stared daggers at Mortimer and spit at him, a glob of protoplasm sailed through Mortimer's face.

"You know, if that had physical form, I'd destroy you now. However, I think that you would be better off in the Nether, cooling your heels for a couple hundred years." Mortimer reached up and rubbed the amulet around his neck breathing onto it. The amulet shimmered and swirled until a portal appeared in front of him. Mortimer pointed to the swirling mass of energy and looked at the young geist. "In.," he ordered.

The geist moved towards the portal and stopped, looking back at Mortimer. The geist flipped him the middle finger, yelling "Screw you pig!" before disappearing into the Nether Realm.

Mortimer watched as the mass dissipated and disappeared. He turned and looked at the older geist. "And you…"

"Hey," said the geist, throwing up his hands. "I tried to

warn him, but he wouldn't listen. Kids his age never do. Nothing but trouble. Too much TV and not enough paddle if you ask me. Spare the rod, spoil the geist, I always say."

"Right," said Mortimer. "If I have to come back here, I'm bringing Bill Murray and Dan Aykroyd and then your fucked, you catch my drift?"

"Not really, no. Who's Bill Murray?" asked the geist but Mortimer didn't wait for a response and stepped out of the house.

Outside, Mortimer sat down on the steps, pulled out a cell phone and called a cab. Why did he never bring any of the teleport powder? He pulled out a cigarette and lit up, letting the smoke glide down his lungs and sighed as he thought about all the paperwork that was ahead of him tonight.

THE GRAVEDIGGER'S APPRENTICE
BY ALEX AZAR

"Forget everything you know about us. We shouldn't even be called gravediggers no more. More like esscavators, cuz thass what we use. No more diggin wit' shovels like we used to."

"Then why do you still carry one around?" John thinks it is an innocent enough question, but Cecil's reaction proves otherwise.

"Why? This job don't end juss cuz the body's inna ground. Lissen Chuck…"

"Name's John."

"You're name's Chuck till I tell you otherwise." Cecil's following statements are more to himself than to anyone, "Damn youngins think they can come n take my job. Hell no! I've been doin this too long." He unzips his pants and rests a hand on a nearby tombstone.

"Whoa, hey old man, what are you doin'?"

"Whass it look like Chucky, bout to drain the dragon." What follows is a sickly laugh hidden behind the cough of a man who's been smoking longer then John's been alive.

"You can't piss on a grave. Don't you care about the people dead here?" John turns, refusing to look at Cecil.

"Lissen youngin, when I started this I cared, but damn long years taught me but one thing. Dead people is dead, and it don't matter one bit if they was good, bad, or pissed on graves; we all rot." Finishing up, Cecil zips up and pats the tombstone, "Ingrid here, she died drunk driving, killing her own daughter. You tellin' me she don't deserve ta get pissed on?"

"Well, um…" stammering for the right answer, "Is that even true?"

"Hell if I know, I don't know bout any o these people

'cept Old Man Higgins top o that hill." The two take a few steps closer but don't actually approach the grave. "He's the oldest stiff here."

"What makes him so special?"

"He died in the war of 1812 and is the only survivor..." more laughing/coughing "...of the original cemetery." Seeing the confused look on John's face, Cecil explains, "The old cemetery ran out of room, so they had to start gettin' rid o people. Slowly but surely over the years, the original class was gone 'cept for Old Man Higgins. See that on his tomb stone?"

John takes a couple steps closer and sees a quick glint of light reflecting off of something bronze. "I see it, what is it?"

"Thass his bell. Back in the day people was buried alive all the time. So's they put these bells with strings on 'em, so if ya woke up down there you could ring the bell." Producing a flask from his pocket-less pants, Cecil continues after a quick swig. "'Cept the damned things so rusted over it ain't rang since 'fore Eisenhower was in the office.

"Matter a fact, next Friday you gotta clean up his site, cuz he's a local hero a couple towns west o here. They the ones that keepin' him round. The Saturday after they're honoring him or something."

That morning Cecil had a fitful sleep, plagued with nightmares of being chased by piss-soaked zombies.

Over the next week each night Cecil gets to work more drunk than the previous night. Until that next Friday night when he arrives more drunk than he is awake. Surprised to see John reporting to work already, "What you doin here so early Chucky?"

"Early? It's after midnight. Our shift starts at 11. Where were you?" Thinking twice about his question and the possible answers, "...better yet, I don't want to know. I'm going to clean Old Man Higgins' site, try not to desecrate anymore graves tonight."

Cecil shoos John away with an uneasy hand, and

formulates that another drink will steady it. Unfortunately, it doesn't. However, the fact that John is on his way to clean the old man's site finally sets in and grants Cecil momentary clarification.

The whole week he's been telling John about the superstitions surrounding graves and cemeteries, and most importantly the bell on Old Man Higgins' tombstone. John had even tested the bell during the day to see if it is indeed rusted over like Cecil claimed. What John didn't know is that Cecil had jammed the hinge and removed the clapper.

While John collected the tools for the job, Cecil rushed to return the clapper and remove the piece of metal jamming the hinge. He waited on the other side of the hill, where he had hidden a line connected to the bell.

Cecil had driven the superstitions far into John's mind, causing him to cautiously approach the tombstone, keeping his eyes focused on the rusted bell. Just a few feet from the tombstone, with the wind at a dead still, the bell rings TANG! Once, twice and a third time, TANG, TANG!

The sudden ringing startled John enough that he let out a yelp of fright and lost his footing, tumbling down the hill. Cecil got to the top in time to hear the thud of John's head smack into Ingrid's tombstone. The sound of a bag of flour slamming into a shallow puddle.

"Oh no, no, no." Cecil runs down the hill, but slows as he sees the dark spot on the tombstone. "Come on Chucky, I'm too drunk for this." He takes a few steps closer, "I'm sorry Chucky, I was juss messin wit you. Wake up Chucky."

Frustrated, scared, and nervous all at once, Cecil throws his flask hitting Phil Carmichael's tombstone. Turning John over, he sees where the back of his head used to be. Instead, he finds a gaping hole filled with brains, bone chips, and blood. Having worked at the cemetery for so long, and a morgue before that, Cecil isn't an easily squeamish person, but this sight combined with his inebriated state plus the knowledge that he caused this was enough to fully turn his stomach.

"That's a good joke Chucky, you got me. I'll even start callin you your real name, but you gotta get up to tell me. The drinkin makes me forget, but I'll even stop drinkin if you get up now."

"What about urinating on grave markers?" Now it was Cecil's turn to stop in his tracks and fall backwards as John gets back to his feet of his own volition.

"Holy shit! You were joking." Cecil places a hand to his chest, physically trying to slow down his heart.

"Please, no cursing in front of ladies." Rising from the grave next to John is a woman in tattered clothing, "You remember Ingrid, right? She did die from a drunk accident like you joked, but it was her husband that was drunk and 'accidentally' choked her too long." Ingrid takes a few steps towards Cecil, "Oh, incidentally, she really hates drunks now." The Ingrid corpse grabs Cecil's arm with impossible strength, tearing into his flesh.

"And Mr. Carmichael doesn't appreciate you using his grave marker as a personal urinal." Carmichael punches Cecil in the face knocking him to the ground. "In fact, none of us do." Cecil looks up to see the cemetery swarmed with the graves' former occupants.

Pulled back to his feet, Cecil sees John before him and in between frightened sobs, "Who are you?"

"You never paid attention to my grave marker, did you? Old Man Higgins died at the age of 19." Extending his hand, "John Higgins, at your service." With that, John grabs Cecil's left ear and rips it off in a single motion.

John turns to address the rest of the horde over Cecil's wails of pain, "Ladies and gentlemen, please don't be avaricious, one piece each, let's make sure there's enough for everyone."

"Brains!"

"Really, Linda? Don't be cliché."

THE BROKEN ANGEL
BY GOLDA MOWE

The day shone bright and clear, giving the gravestones, grasses and leaves a washed look. It was a perfect day for a picnic, yet standing not twenty yards away from Tomlin was a silent group of grey and black mourners encircling a simple polished coffin. After a few moments of silence, the funeral director, a portly ruddy checked man, hooked three cables to a hydraulic hoist and lifted the coffin up to lower it down again into a freshly dug hole next to it. Once it was safely interned inside, he urged the mourners to return with him to the funeral home and they left the site. Tomlin shuffled towards the hole and began to shovel in clay dirt.

"Hello there, Tom," a voice called out from behind him.

Tomlin turned and saw a man dressed in a dog suit. He looked like a brown beagle with a heart shaped patch over his belly and chest.

"What do you want?" Tomlin asked.

"I'm here to remind you to save the girl," said Dog-man.

Tomlin turned back to his work. "She's dead. Mr. Doyle said so in his speech just now. I have to bury her."

"Are you sure? Have you checked?"

"Yes, I am sure, and no, I don't have to check."

"Well, open the coffin and see. You don't want to end up burying someone alive do you?"

Tomlin paused and stared at the lush foliage of a sycamore tree in the distance. Then as though having made up his mind, he planted the shovel into the mound of dirt and slipped down into the hole. He scraped off dirt from the upper cover then using a crowbar hanging from his tool belt, he pried the cover open. Inside lay a teenage girl, porcelain pale with her hands clasped chastely over her chest.

"See," Dog-man said, "I told you she is still alive."

Tomlin reached down into the coffin and pulled her out. He slung the cold body over his shoulder and climbed out. After propping her into a sitting position against a gravestone, he returned to his work of shoveling dirt into the hole. Dog-man sat next to the girl and watched him.

An old couple walked past them, carrying an armful of red carnations between them. A few minutes later the funeral director returned just as he was beginning to slap down the dirt with his shovel to pack them down.

"Tom," the man said, "I need you to dig another one down by the old mausoleum."

"But all the spots have been filled up, Mr. Doyle."

Doyle released a heavy sigh. "No, there are still two more available spots. Dig out George Baker. He doesn't have any family around these parts anyway, so no one will notice. Take him back to the house as usual."

"Yes, sir."

Doyle turned and spotted the girl. He let out another sigh. "You really shouldn't leave her out in the open like that, Tom. Someone might see."

"But she is still alive. Nobody is going to mind even if they see."

Doyle shrugged. "As long as you remember to take her back to the house. Last time you forgot to bring the boy in and he was left out here all afternoon."

"I won't forget this time, I promise. Anyway, Dog-man is here to remind me."

"Hmm, very well," Doyle said after one final look at the solitary girl. "Tell Dog-man to keep this secret to himself. The last thing we want is for people to send all their loved ones to William's Cemetery."

"Yes, sir. Me and Dog-man's mouths are sealed."

Doyle waved to the returning old couple with a smile, and when they made to turn his way, he hurried over to their side and walked with them down a well-trodden path towards the parking space.

Once they were out of sight, Tomlin put down his shovel and picked up the girl. He wound his way deeper into the cemetery, towards an old 3-storey building at the edges of the burial site. He passed through a low picket gate that linked the well-kept hedge encircling the house. Instead of walking up the main path to the front door, he turned down a dirt trail leading to the side of the house. He heaved open the basement door with one hand and trudged down the steps.

The photographer Casey was already there, busily setting up a background screen of winter woodland and two studio lights. Tomlin lay the girl down on a threadbare sofa by the side then sat down on the open cushion space by her feet.

Soon Casey approached and Tom helped him prop her up against a stand. Doyle's embalming work was so perfect that her body had remained supple and her skin unblemished. Casey cut the fabric of her clothing with a pair of scissors and stripped her nude. He lifted her chin a little and placed her hands to the side. Then he switched on the studio lights and began to take pictures. Every now and then he would put down his camera and move her, change her position or tease her hair but always he would pose her in ways that highlight her perfect youth.

Into the second hour of their photo shoot, Doyle came down from the house above. "Any problems?" he asked.

"Nope," Casey said, "She is perfect. I can sell these pictures easy."

"Good," Doyle said, "That will make up for the discount I gave her parents."

Casey chuckled. "More than make up for it, I'll say."

Doyle turned to Tomlin and said, "Good job, Tom. You have saved her life. Now we can send her to heaven, where she will be happy forever."

Tomlin gurgled with joy. As Casey put away his equipment and switched off the lights, Tomlin again picked up the girl and put her into a box which had been placed atop a sliding rack. Casey put her clothes and shoes on her belly. Then Doyle slid the box into the furnace and fired it up.

The early evening shadows outside was long by the time Tomlin returned to her grave to retrieve his shovel and to drag the hoist away with him. He went straight to Baker's grave where Dog-man was already waiting.

"Are you going to dig him up tonight?"

"Yes, someone else needs the ground." Tom thrust his shovel into the ground and stepped on the top edges to drive it farther into the clay.

"Must be someone important," Dog-man said.

"I guess so. Mr. Doyle only gives these spots to important people."

"Why is that you think?"

Tom shrugged. "This was the old church ground. When my grandfather sold it to Mr. Doyle, there were only six graves here, and he made Mr. Doyle promise to never dig any of them up. Now there is only Baker and that other nameless one left."

"You mean the other four are no longer here?"

"Yes. Friedman, Burns, Roastville and Carver. Grandfather made me remember all their names."

Dog-man laughed. "They sound like a cooking class."

Tomlin eased off his digging to look up. "I guess so."

"Then the person in the middle must be Chef Nameless."

Again the shovel crunched through the hard ground. "Maybe. It makes sense."

Dog-man watched silently from the side.

Casey shook his head as he trudged past the mausoleum with Doyle. "There he goes, talking to himself again."

"Don't be too hard on him. As long as his imaginary friend is okay with what we are doing, we'll get along fine."

"How in the world did you ever get to persuade him that all those kids were still alive?"

"I didn't. His imaginary friend figured it for him." A pause. "Did you remember to take a face portrait for him?"

"Yes, the usual. Why not give him a full nude?"

"He doesn't like those. He's only interested in their sleeping faces."

Casey released a snort. "Will you be needing me anytime soon?"

"No. Going somewhere?" Doyle asked.

"Yeh. After I upload these photos, I'm going to the Caribbean with a living woman."

"Good for you. I don't expect anything anytime soon. So enjoy yourself."

Casey stepped into the car park of the funeral home and went straight to his car while Doyle made his way to the single story building. Just as he unlocked the door, Casey honked and flashed his lights before driving off. Doyle waved in return then went into the preparation room to take out an industrial-sized hand truck before returning to the mausoleum.

By the time he had hauled the equipment to the grave site, Tomlin had reached the iron casket lying in a bed of salt. Doyle sniffed. For the life of him, he couldn't understand why anyone would want to bury a rotting corpse inside a perpetual box. Tomlin climbed out of the hole and positioned the arm of the hoist over the grave. Then he went down again and Doyle threw three chains after him. Doyle watched with a little apprehension and amazement as Tomlin slung the chains under the casket at three points with just the crowbar as his lever.

When the day grew so dim that Doyle had to switch on a flashlight, Tomlin again climbed out of the hole and turned the wheel of the hoist. The chains snapped taut. Slowly the casket rose. Once he had lifted it over the edges of the hole, Tomlin turned another wheel and swung it to the side. Doyle positioned the reclined hand-truck under it as Tomlin lowered it slowly. Once it was securely on the hand truck, Doyle released the chain. Tomlin grasped the handle of the hand truck and heaved it up with a loud shout before pushing it ahead of him back to the house.

Doyle went ahead of him to unlock the door to the wide elevator leading down to the basement. Once there, Tomlin lowered the handles and pushed one end of the casket to the floor. Then he heaved the side of the hand truck and slid the whole casket to the floor with a loud clang. He dragged the hand truck back to the elevator and returned to the dug grave. After tidying up the area and sending the hoist back to the funeral home, he returned to the house and found Doyle waiting for him by the side of the furnace.

Again Tomlin reached for his crowbar and pried the casket open. They lowered the heavy cover to the side and exposed a well preserved body that had shrunken down to a skeletal frame. Tomlin picked it up and placed it on the furnace rack. Doyle pushed it into the furnace and set it afire.

"Good job, Tom. I've got a steak dinner ready for you. After you finish eating, help me clean up this coffin, okay."

"Yes, Mr. Doyle, sir."

Doyle smiled benevolently and patted his shoulder before climbing up the stairs to the house above. The lock upstairs clanged as he bolted the door.

Tomlin shuffled to the table and ate his dinner with his soiled hands. Outside a storm began to brew. After he finished dinner, he sent the plate to the sink. Then he went to the coffin and scrubbed the bare interior clean. Once that was done, he scrubbed the cover and outside surface. Finally he buffed it with grease, giving its dark surface a high gloss. It was late and he was tired by the time he was done and had left the basement.

Dog-man said, "Don't forget to lock the door."

Tomlin turned back and snapped on the padlock. "Thanks for reminding me."

"No problem, pal. Let's go home."

They made straight for the mausoleum. Tomlin unlatched the heavy door and once inside he pulled out a worn single mattress hidden behind a sarcophagus and placed it atop the flat stone lid. Then he climbed up and went to sleep. Dog-man sat at the open doorway and watched the nameless grave outside.

The night grew colder and darker and from a distant town hall, the clock struck three. The earth began to move. Soon a hand appeared from under its surface, followed by an arm and another hand. Dog-man crawled on all fours to the side of the grave. A head appeared.

"Master," Dog-man said, "You have returned."

The master heaved himself out of the hole and breathed in deep. He chortled. "Yes, I have. Where is my broken angel?"

"Tom is here. I have looked after him for you."

"Thank you, old friend. I am starving though."

"You will find a good meal in the old house; asleep, alone and awash with the gravy of his own vileness."

Nameless licked his lips then quick as lightning he jumped into the air and flew to the house.

Dog-man waited an hour or so. He sniffed the air, turned back to the mausoleum and shook Tomlin's shoulder. "Tom, we must go to the house. The master calls us."

Tomlin sat up and rubbed his eyes. "Okay," he mumbled before following Dog-man back to the house. As he climbed the last step to the porch, he realized with a start that he was standing at the front door. He turned.

Dog-man said, "Where are you going?"

"To the basement door. Mr. Doyle doesn't like me on his porch. He will be mad if he sees me here."

"It's okay, Tom. The old house master has returned. He won't mind you using his front door."

As Tom stood there undecided, the door open and a tall bearded thin man said, "Why are you two standing out here in the cold. Come in. Supper is ready."

Timidly Tom followed Dog-man into the house. It was spotless and filled with shiny objects, making him stare about him with wonder. He stumbled his way into the dining room and sat down at the edge of a chair that the master indicated to him. Spread out on the table were tomato soup, roast meat, cold cut salad, baked bread and a special brown gravy by the side.

Tom slurped down the soup served to him hungrily but stopped when he felt something hard rolling in his mouth. He fished it out – a ring. "Look!" he said gleefully, "Mr. Doyle's ring. Can I keep it?"

Nameless said, "Of course you may. It is yours now."

Tom put it on his little finger, a perfect fit. They continued their meal until dawn broke through the horizon. Then Tom was told to go to his childhood room where he slept until late noon. And when he woke, there was a meal waiting.

LOGAN WILLIAMS, AGENT OF S.P.A.R.C.
BY JASON T. COUNTRYMAN

Logan woke with a start. His dreams were getting worse. It had been years since his time in the Special Paranormal Action and Research Commission, cleaning up all the messes and leftovers from various paranormal phenomena and ethereal events that the rank and file citizenry had no knowledge of. Helping to draw the line between the good people of society and the things that go bump in the night.

Logan's days were easier now. Being the sole funeral home and mortician business in the large rural area afforded certain benefits. He was affluent enough, a respected member of the community, and a civic leader. For Logan, though, it was all a house of cards. An elaborate cover. Underneath the elegant suit during a funeral service or the local high school's team colors while volunteering at the concession stand, Logan would be eternally conflicted.

His dreams would subside, for weeks or months at a time. His usual clients were the elderly or the infirm. People that had died peacefully. Prep work for them was easy. It was the accidents that would bring the dreams rushing back. A farmer mangled while working on a harvester. A teenager that didn't make the turn on a back-country road in time. Every mutilated body that he serviced as the undertaker/funeral director brought waves of memories crashing against the shores of his mind. Opening a body bag and seeing the dismembered remains of an accident at the paper mill would guarantee a week of shattered sleep, punctuated by terrifying nightmares.

Old Man Kowalski had been driving his pickup along

County Route 5, to his farm that lay out near the end of the Ashland Road. It was early morning. He had been into the Kwik Stop in the village to grab a coffee, the paper, and a treat for Angus, his yellow lab mix that always accompanied him on the trip in the morning.

County Route 5 is a little out-of-the-way even for a small town, but it still gets snowplowed when needed. On this cold morning, it was needed. An overnight snowfall had coated the road with a thin layer of wet snow. The cloudless day ahead and temperatures forecast to stay just below freezing called for the snowplows to get out early, before the layer of snow turned into a layer of ice from the sun.

Kowalski never saw the snowplow barreling down upon him. It happened where County Route 5 splits off and becomes the Ashland Road on the left fork, and stays County Route 5 on the right. The snowplow driver, having suffered a stroke just seconds before, couldn't heed the stop sign at the end of the right fork.

The snowplow severed the truck in two. The blade from the plow entered the passenger side door. Angus was killed immediately. The blade continued through the cab in a diagonal orientation towards the rear of the truck. It missed Kowalski proper, but sheared the seat away from him as the remainder of the plow truck tore through the pickup.

The two pieces of pickup spun away from the plow as it continued on through and finally came to a stop when the front wheels cleared the shoulder and dove into the deep ditch below. Kowalski, not dead yet, was thrown from the spinning cab of the pickup. He catapulted through where the seat would have been behind him directly towards the barbed-wire fence that lay beyond the ditch. The fence post entered just below his right shoulder blade, ran out the top of his collarbone and entered his head underneath his chin. The force from the collision nearly doubled over the fence post, but wasn't enough to push the post out through his skull. His limbs, thankfully lifeless at this point, tangled in the barbed-wire. His face was frozen in a look of utter shock. Or it might have just been the fence post propping his mouth open.

Logan was sitting with his normal Saturday morning coffee crew at the downtown diner. Creekside Diner was a small dining room, counter, and kitchen attached to the remains of an inn. The food wasn't good and the service was worse. But the coffee was hot and cheap. Joining Logan this morning were the High School P.E. teacher and Varsity Basketball coach, the owner of the liquor/hardware store, and the owner of Creekside. The discussion had turned to the new quarterback for Syracuse University when Kowalski's truck rumbled by unnoticed.

It was the screaming siren and lights of the first responders as their vehicles accelerated past the street-facing windows of the diner that captured the group's attention several minutes later. They turned their gaze to the street as a green Ford pickup with a blue light, the Sheriff's light-blue and white sedan, and the volunteer ambulance rumbled by.

"That's an awful lot of noise they're stirring up out there", Creekside's owner offered.

"Always is.", was Logan's reply.

The group turned back to their discussion. Twenty minutes later, Logan's cellphone began to ring. Excusing himself from the group after putting a five dollar bill in the tip jar, Logan moved outside to quickly get the best signal before answering. The conversation was simple enough. He needed to, as the only undertaker vetted by the town board, head to the Ashland Rd. to pick up a couple bodies.

The flashing lights from the emergency vehicles welcomed Logan to the scene. He slowed the 20 year old GMC Jimmy down to a near crawl as he navigated through the throng of onlookers. His transmission slipping from upper to lower gears roughly, adding a physical shudder to the emotional one already at work in Logan's psyche. The first responders had already cordoned off the area, and were standing around the wreckage of the pickup. It looked like one of them was being violently ill. The plow driver's body had already been placed into a body bag. Kowalski still hung suspended in his current resting place.

"Shit, this is going to be a long day", Logan said as he rounded the wreckage of the rear of the truck and saw Sheriff Wilson inspecting what looked to be the actual point of impact between the two vehicles.

"Yeah, the first responder said we've got 2 casualties, both dead on impact.", Sheriff Wilson remarked before standing slowly and turning to Logan, "I'm not sure he's right about the plow driver. There's no real bruising around the impact sites where his head met the steering wheel. And the dash. I think he was dead before."

"Heart attack or stroke, you think?" Logan asked.

"Your guess is as good as mine. Do what you have to do to collect Kowalski's body, then I need you out of here as soon as possible."

"Sounds good."

Logan dropped the seats of the Jimmy and piled in the body of the plow driver on his own. Kowalski required some help. A reciprocating saw and some determination got the fence post down.

Later that day, Logan was working on the bodies in his small lab. Logan started with the unenviable task of removing a metal fence post. He decided that instead of removing the post from the torso itself, he would cut the exposed pieces of the post off. That would leave the piece of the post still inside the body between the shoulder blade and the collarbone. The piece penetrating the neck offered the same opportunity. Logan forced the mouth closed, to make sure it would. Satisfied, he pulled out the fence post from the bottom ever so slightly. The saw made quick work of the end, and the remaining post slid back into the skull easily.

Happy with the outcome, Logan was sure that he could work with the corpse in this condition. You couldn't see any traces of the fence post, and all it would take is a quick staple and a tight collar to hide the entrance wound in the neck.

As he turned to begin processing the plow driver, Logan heard a rap-rap-rap at the basement doors. Opening the wide double-doors, Sheriff Wilson greeted him with an awkward smile and a child's body bag.

"Family of the old man requested that he be accompanied by this," Wilson said as he handed Logan the bag.

"I told them I'm sure you'd be able to handle it. Not like it's the first weird request us hicks have given you."

Logan looked at the sheriff quizzically. He motioned Wilson to follow him as he retreated back into the lab. Logan secured the bag on the free stainless steel table and turned to Wilson as he grabbed the zipper.

"Interest you in some coffee, Sheriff?" Logan looked up, hoping the Sheriff would decline and leave him to his work.

"No, sir, and I don't figure you'll be wanting any either once you open that bag."

Intrigued, Logan refocused on the zipper and pulled down quickly. He got to see the nearly decapitated yellow lab. The head only held on by a few thin strands of flesh covered by tan fur.

The memories came flooding back. They assaulted his mind, as if punches from a boxer, each one more powerful than the next.

He straightened bolt upright, and yelled out.

"RUN!! RUUUNNNNNNNNN!!!!"

The dreams had started while he was still with the Mitigation and Recovery Division. His days were filled with autopsies, necropsies, dissections, all manner of research into things gory and best left in the realm of make-believe. He had no shortage of images and memories remaining to fuel a lifetime of dreams.

It was the re-animations that bothered Logan the most. He could still see them when he closed his eyes, those dismembered bodies, evidence of grand battles won (or sometimes lost) by the Action Response Division. Logan was one of the best researchers in M and R, but the thought of zombies, in any form, scared him beyond any rational explanation.

It is the very nature of zombies, or "Sloppies" as commonly referred to in the Commission, to be VERY hard to kill. It usually took a complete dismemberment; the head far away from the body so that the arms, in their few minutes of flailing about, couldn't find the head and shove it back onto the body. It was an encounter with a particularly nasty Sloppy (so named for their second life, which the grunts in the Action Response Division considered the corpse's "Sloppy Seconds") that prompted Logan to leave the commission. To escape into a normal life.

There had been a re-animation event in Northern New York, near the Canadian border. First reports were simple enough cases of what looked like rabies among a bat population on a small peninsula into Lake Ontario called Three Mile Point. S.P.A.R.C. didn't get dispatched until one of the local populace was bitten and it was quickly determined that it wasn't rabies.

Patient Zero was a man in his late 30s that lived on the peninsula. He had tried to remove an infected bat from the loft of his garage with a tennis racket. He succeeded, but was bitten. His wife watched his body die from the infection in mere seconds before the volunteer ambulance squad had even made it to the scene.

Patient Zero re-animated while the squad was trying to revive him. He wiped out the entire group, including his wife and dog. Of the 6 casualties (counting the dog), 4 were re-animated themselves.

The Action Response Division efficiently quelled the

disturbance. Logan wasn't a fan of the men in A and R, but they were good at what they did. Even still, Sloppies are hard to kill.

Mitigation and Recovery followed on the scene no less than five minutes after the last confirmed re-kill. Speed was necessary in these cases, to keep the populace in the dark about things too terrifying to know. Logan came upon the canine first. It actually seemed to be in pretty good condition, with most of its flesh and skin intact. The head lay a meter or so beyond, the lower jaw partially removed, and an obvious hole where Patient Zero had attacked it while it was still living, trying to get to the gray matter of its brain.

Normal procedure was to bag the body and head separately. Logan knew this. It was second nature to him, after 6 years with M and R. It wasn't second nature to the new trainee, Agent Deal. Young and fresh from college, Deal was recruited for her research ability and skill with autopsy. Deal was also extremely fascinated with the Sloppies, and very eager to examine them.

This was Deal's first excursion, and her excitement made her stick out. She made it to the canine's head first, while Logan was crouched over the body still checking for signs of lingering animation. There was no way she could have seen the snakelike tendrils of flesh still reaching out from the neck trying to reach the head. Logan figured, by the thickness and length of the tendrils, this body had three to five minutes of re-animation left without the head.

Deal nodded to Logan, "What do you make of the injury to the jaw?" she asked. Logan looked up in time to see the just-thrown head nearing him in the air. His fear response kicked in. Logan knew that if the tendrils could reach the head, the zombie canine would become a threat again.

Logan yelled out, "RUN! RUUUNNNNNNNNNN!!!!"

Deal stood, stunned.

Logan didn't see the neck and head reattach, with the head slightly off-kilter. Logan didn't watch the dog attack

Deal as it buried its teeth into Deal's throat. It all happened over the span of a heartbeat.

Logan was running.

Logan couldn't know that the infected saliva entered Deal's bloodstream through the bite in her neck. The virus, for lack of a better term, coursed through her veins, replicating rapidly. The virus needed a specific, but not rare, genetic marker in a host's body that caused a release of a unique flavor of dopamine. Once the virus reached the *substantia nigra* structure in the victim's brain, the virus's dopamine receptors were engaged. This allowed the virus to produce the unknown hormone that triggered the death and re-animation chain reaction which destroyed the victim's consciousness. The hormone remained resident only in the victim's brain. Therefore, transmission of the hormone was not possible from attacker to victim, only the virus.

The A and R escort shot Deal through the forehead as the virus reached the dopamine production center, stopping the chain reaction before it could take hold completely inside her body.

Logan didn't know.

Logan was running.

Logan had no idea that the other A and R escort had decapitated the dog almost immediately.

Logan was still running.

He could see the dog behind him in his mind. Could see the hunger in its eyes. He ran. Screaming.

It was the laughter from the escort that brought him back to sanity. The laughter was almost evil. Logan slowed down, realized that he had been squealing from the hoarseness in his breath. He could hear the A and R escort yelling out, "Hey, did everyone see Logan's Run?! Baaahahahhhahhaaa!"

When Logan finally awoke, his first image was of Sheriff Wilson standing over him.

"Good Lord, man, what was that all about? I damn near shit myself."

"What happened?" Logan was still fuzzy.

"Well, you opened that friggin' bag, yelled 'Run!' and then passed out. You scared the piss outta me". Sheriff Wilson did not seem amused.

"Right, the dog…" Logan trailed off in a hoarse half-whisper.

"Yeah, the dog. What the fuck is wrong with you?"

"Bad dreams, Sheriff…bad dreams."

FEEDING THE SOIL
BY LIAM CADEY

Historically, the Havant family had ferried the majority of the parish's inhabitants into the soil in as dignified and respectable a way as possible but, in the cut and thrust world of modern life, it seemed that people now preferred less costly and more discreet ways to ship off their loved ones.

Brian, the last of the Havant line and sole operative of the business, stood to one side of the graveyard, pruning the last of the season's roses, while the immaculate but inappropriately dressed widow who stood by the open grave seemed more concerned with trying to prevent the breeze from spoiling her good looks.

Her husband had been brought to Brian by the smooth city type who now stood waiting by her Mercedes at the front of the church. The man had brought a grin, a change of clothes, some ugly personal jewellery, and instructions that he use the cheapest coffin that he could find.

His father had often said, over an evening's whisky or two, that the coffin said more about the family than the deceased.

All that he had to do, after carefully checking the death certificate and making sure that all the formalities had been followed, was to tidy up and present his customer, dig a hole and bury him – and even those efforts seemed wasted, as she had only cast a cursory glance at the person who had been her husband.

Times were indeed hard, as were wives, it seemed.

Having said all that needed to be said, the priest paused for a few reflective moments, before addressing the woman.

"Mrs. Kunster, rest assured that your husband's resting place will receive only the best treatment," he glanced meaningfully towards the middle-aged man dressed in a tired, greying suit, and swept the graveyard with a delicate hand. "Mr. Havant and his family have generations of experience, as you can see."

The bored widow didn't seem to be that bothered, and barely acknowledged Brian, the verdant grass paths, the abundant flower beds, the well-tended and carefully cleaned graves or even the artfully pruned trees that gave the graveyard its reputation as the place to be - eventually, of course.

After ignoring a few more words of consolation, she made her way back to the car. Brian waited until she was out of sight before taking a swig from the small hipflask he always kept on his person; it was a habit that he had picked up from his father, but he kept to a limit of one flask a day.

"She's a cool character, isn't she, Mr. Pembleton sir?" Brian nodded towards the front of the church, while lighting up a hand rolled cigarette.

"As you may know, Mr. Havant, the loss of a loved one is a challenging time for everyone, and people deal with it in their own way," the young but already balding priest glanced disapprovingly at the limp cigarette. "I'll leave it to you to see that things are sorted out."

Without further ado, Pembleton made his way to the front of the church, and sound of his Land Rover was quickly smothered by the surrounding woodland. Silence once again fell over Calborn church and its grounds.

Brian savoured the cigarette, the warm smoke mixing pleasantly with the earthy, autumnal air. It was the first time that he had met the parish priest in person as most contact was made over the telephone, but it was evident that the new boy lacked a sense of humour; Jacobson, the previous priest, had understood the dark side of life but had liked his drink too much, which was probably why he'd had to bury the old chap a few months ago.

His small cottage stood to one side of the church grounds, and he returned there to change into his normal work clothes, rather than the presentable set he wore for guests. Standing in front of the mirror, buttoning up his tattered overalls and ignoring the increasing amount of grey that flecked his hair, he wondered how much work he had left; it came to him sporadically now, and vary rarely did he do more than simple dress and bury jobs.

Calborn church and its parish had the fortune of being located at the edge of the craggy north Devon coast, trapped on three sides by the rocky, tree encrusted slopes of the moors and to the front by the unforgiving Bristol Channel. The little flat land that existed at the bottom of the valley was taken up by the church, its grounds, and the farm whose land ran down to the cold sea. The extreme topography of the region had helped remove it from the eyes of hungry developers – but he knew that its isolation would inevitably lead to its demise, as people left the area.

The church only required his services because he was a cheap caretaker. He not only performed the duties of a funeral director for his own ends, but also maintained the church, its grounds and several others in the area as a top-up on his income. He owned the dilapidated family cottage and the small stone building opposite, where his business was conducted; fed himself from the large vegetable garden that he maintained, and topped it up with any small game that he could poach from the surrounding woodland.

But as he made his way back to the grave he knew, with a little warm pride, that it was the level of care that he put into the ground's maintenance that really made him useful to the cash-strapped but appearance-conscious Church: the intricately carved wooden lichgate, now almost too small for the current generation, was in good repair, the paving that ran through the graveyard was weed-free and level, flower borders were well planned and bright throughout the entire growing season and even the headstones and markers were moss and lichen free.

On reaching the grave, he dropped his tools and taking

care, lowered himself into the hole and opened the top-half of the lid. He had chosen a stable-door style coffin, because it made accessing it a little easier whilst standing in the grave.

He noted that the powdered features of Mr. Kunster seemed relatively relaxed, but judging by the wife's cool exterior, he wouldn't have been surprised if that had come after his death; he also realised that the hubby seemed a lot older too.

Brian removed the man's watch, cufflinks and the other petty valuables, while keeping an ear open for any possible visitors.

His father had always insisted on keeping the soil clean and free from artificial materials, and Brian reasoned that the least he could do was keep up the family tradition.

As usual, after he had filled in the grave, the rest of the day passed quickly: Pembleton supplied him with a constant supply of odd jobs, which appeared with a regularity that showed he was intent on getting the parish up to scratch and building up a reputation for himself – and while it grated on Brian that the Church just didn't appreciate what his family had put into the soil, he enjoyed his job too much to complain.

***

"Brian, you'll be at Calborn later in the afternoon, won't you?" The priest sounded grave, more than normal, anyway.

"Yes, Mr. Pembleton, I'll be here," he sighed, all too used to these calls. "What do you need me to do?"

"It would seem that Mrs. Bergkopf may have been a little pre-emptive, shall we say, in burying her late husband," Pembleton paused, "the enquiry has been reopened and permission to exhume granted."

"That's unusual sir. Exhume, did you say?" There was malicious gossip and rumour in the locality, as there was in all places, but never taken to this level.

"Yes, Mr. Havant."

"But there'll be nothing left, if you'll forgive me saying

so," he tried to stall.

"What do you mean?"

"What I mean is, sir, is that the area has wild rats, and they don't need much time," he was thinking fast. "What with not being allowed to use poison, they live underground, and there's nothing that me or old Scrumpy, my cat, can do about them."

"I've never heard of such a thing. But anyway, Mr. Havant, it has already been decided and while I do agree that it is unusual, this is beyond my control; the rats are something that we can deal with, if necessary, at a later date," the younger man paused, awaiting further resistance, but Brian knew he couldn't give any.

"I suppose it has to be, then."

"Thank you Brian, and yes, I know that this is always a disappointment, but it brings us down to earth, I suppose," he conceded. "Three it is then. And I'll let you deal with them." The click of the receiver being replaced ended the conversation.

The rest of the morning passed painfully slowly as he considered the possibility that someone would miss the dead man's missing items, and he hadn't even had the time to pawn them yet. He was so deep in thought and focused on trimming the Hazel hedge that prevented the sea wind from scouring the graveyard, that he didn't hear the contractors until they shouted introductions from the front of the church; when he called out a greeting in reply, they came around to the rear of the church.

"Quite a place you've got here," stated the older of the dungaree clad pair, after they had shaken hands with Brian. "I'm Arnold, and this is Jez," he indicated his younger and less well-padded companion.

"We could do with working in a place like this, couldn't we lad, with all this fresh air and scenery," Arnold continued, breathing deeply and surveying the rolling landscape, now tinged with autumn gold.

"Wouldn't be very quiet though," his companion added, "with you talking all the time."

"Cheeky bastard," Arnold scanned the orderly Church Grounds. "It's going to be a shame to dig a hole in this place, you've done a real good job," he acknowledged. "Where's the victim then?"

"It isn't going to be worth your effort, gentlemen," Brian pointed to the grave when they looked at him quizzically. "Rats, there'll be nothing left."

"I've seen some things in my time mate, but I've never heard of rats," Arnold shook his head.

"It'll be alright, it's only been two weeks since you put him in," added Jez, digging in his spade. "The ground's not boggy and it hasn't rained for a while, so the box should still be solid. We won't even have to look at the poor sod."

Brian had no choice but to watch them work, and so lit a roll-up to pass the time, watching the pair make rapid progress in the soft, loamy soil.

"My misses would love this stuff," Arnold lifted a handful of dark earth, breathing a little deeply from the exertion, "good for the garden."

"She deals with the garden, you deal with the birds, eh?" his companion added.

"That's right son, now put your back to it." For the next few minutes, the subtle sound of the countryside around them was broken only by the crunching of sliced soil and pattering earth. Brian rolled another cigarette and hoped that they would just take the coffin, and not check its inhabitant; that way the blame could be spread if any questions did arise.

A hollow crunching sound came from the deepening hole, and the young worker swore, a little effeminately.

"For god's sake be careful," the older man stopped digging, wiped his sweaty brow with a dirty sleeve and bent down out of sight, his bald head reappearing seconds later.

"Well, I can see how you could put your foot through it, the bloody wood's rotten," he looked at his companion, "and stinks too. Now get out of the way. I'll do it myself and we'll work something out."

Brian helped pull Jez out, who spent a few moments studying his muddy boot, while the older man cleared the remaining soil off the top of the coffin; when he had finished, Jez and a reluctant Brian moved forward. The hole through which the younger workman had put his foot was at the foot of the coffin, and was pitch black in the poor light of the grave; but the stench which emanated from it was evident, even from ground level.

"Can we get it out in one piece?" Brian asked hopefully.

"Best not, it'll probably break and then we'll be in even more trouble," Arnold took hold of his spade, wedged it under the lid and forced it up with ease.

Brian felt a moment's panic as he realised that he'd forgotten to lock it again.

But that was the last thing that Arnold was bothered about, as he staggered back, his skin suddenly a shade paler. Jez leant forward so see more clearly, and then threw up into the grave, spattering his colleague's trousers.

Mr. Kunster's eyes had gone, as had most of the flesh on his head, torso and arms; the bones, where they were still intact, gleamed sickly under the layer of greyish slime that coated the remains and pooled at the bottom of the coffin, itself riddled with holes; a fishy and cloying miasma rose from coffin's contents, some of which writhed in slippery, greasy coils.

Even Brian, whose father had detailed the work of the strange worms that their great-grandfather had brought back from his sailing days, was taken aback a little, and took an involuntary drag on his cigarette that was so strong it almost scorched his tongue.

He'd hoped they would have finished by now, but the man-made fibres of the corpse's cheap clothing must have delayed their work, and he realised that he only had one chance to keep the family secret.

"Do you see what I mean?" He asked the men, as they were trying to pull themselves together a little. "Shall we say the rats got him?"

"What the hell are..." the spade caught Arnold under the chin before he could finish, and despite the age gap, Brian managed to finish off a stunned Jez before he could wipe the vomit from his lips.

When silence had once again fallen over the church and its grounds, Brian took a swig from his flask, smoked a cigarette, and took a few minutes to ponder his future; but surrounded by the colourful late blooms and fruit-bearing trees, all of which were a product of the rapid, soil-improving processes of the worms, he realised he didn't have a choice.

He picked up his spade and started shoveling.

Winter was coming and he'd have to feed the earth well if he wanted to stay in business, and he was lucky to have some fresh composting material to work with; and with any luck, glancing up at the cloud-streaked sky, he could make a start on repairing the old hiker's path that ran past the church.

A business had to meet its running costs, after all.

JUST A TASTE
BY MATT NORD

Rebecca stood over the corpse, a middle-aged man that she did not know. He was from the same town she lived in, but she still had no idea who he was. Rebecca didn't get out much. She spent most of her time pouring over any books she could get her hands on (mainly ordered online; libraries and book stores required too much human contact) or simply lying in bed listening to classical music. She preferred Mahler, an Austrian composer born in the late nineteenth century. Her favorite works of his were the Kindertotenlieder. The melodies came beautifully out of the antique phonograph she had been fortunate enough to find at a relatively secluded shop one unusual day. Unusual in the fact that she was outside of her house and the sun had actually been out.

She didn't own a television, or she would probably sit in front of it for hours on end, pondering how so many people could stand being around each other for so long. This lack of the modern form of entertainment was a holdover from her parents, both of whom were clinical technophobes. No cell phones, no computers, no television. It was surprising to those who had known them that they even owned a car.

She gazed down at the graying body that lay before her and let out a sigh. It was only a matter of time before it spoke to her. And when it finally did speak, it would be the same as it always had been.

The dead had not always talked to Rebecca Mossier. It hadn't started until around her eleventh birthday, around the time she reached puberty. It also didn't always happen when it did start. The first time a dead person talked to her was at her paternal grandmother's funeral. She had never been to one before. No dead relatives (that they were close to, anyway), no dead pets. In fact, she had never seen a dead body of any sort, barring the dead flies she used to find in the windowsills of her house. She liked to pick them up and crush their dead, dried bodies between her index finger and thumb, smashing them into a fine powder before blowing them away into oblivion.

On the day of her first funeral, she had been standing with her father and mother before anyone had arrived at the funeral home. They had been talking with the funeral director about some last minute preparations as she stood silently holding her mother's hand like the good little girl they had raised her to be.

Her parents and the funeral director, Mr. Smith or Schmidt or something like that, talked for quite some time and Rebecca began to grow bored. Her mind began to wander before she heard a voice call to her.

"Rebecca," the soft, elderly voice said. She looked up at her parents. Neither of them was looking at her, and it certainly hadn't been Mr. Smith/Schmidt, although he was rather old and he did speak with a very subdued voice. The adults continued on with their conversation as if they hadn't heard anything.

"Rebecca," she heard again. "Come over here."

She looked around the parlor of the funeral home, not seeing another living soul besides her, her parents and the funeral director. She let go of her mother's hand, the woman seeming not to notice, and slowly drifted away from her parents.

Again she looked all around the parlor trying to determine the source of the command. And again she saw no one. There were only the three adults and her and…

"That's right, sweetie," Rebecca heard, "come to Nanna."

She felt a lump form in her throat as she stopped dead in tracks. Breaking out in gooseflesh Rebecca cast a glance back at her parents. They continued their conversation with the funeral director as if nothing were out of the ordinary.

"Come here, Rebecca," came the voice from inside the open casket. She felt compelled to obey. It was, after all, her Nanna.

Rebecca shuffled her white patent leather shoes along the awful looking orangish-brown carpet toward her grandmother's casket. She kept her eyes straight ahead, keeping them focused on a point on the wall just above the casket. As she reached the end of the clothed-lined pine box, she was assaulted by the overwhelming smells of powder, makeup and hairspray, along with something else she couldn't quite place. Like cough drops or something her mother would rub on her chest when she had a bad cold.

Her parents never used actually medicine, or a doctor for that matter, but would sometimes employ herbal remedies or mildly medicinal anointing oils. As members of a radical sect of the Church of Christian Science, they believed that illnesses should be combated with prayer, not drugs or other means of man. A lack of faith in the healing power of Christ was considered heretical and would result in excommunication.

They had instilled upon her a healthy respect for Jesus and the power that He possesses, including the power to raise the dead. *Lord, make me not afraid,* the young girl thought.

Rebecca closed her eyes and took a deep breath. Letting it out, she looked down at her very much dead grandmother. Her ancient skin looked like wrinkled paper covered with too much makeup. The bright blue shaded eyelids were closed, her mouth still, her breathing naught.

Had she just been hearing things? Was she somehow projecting her own wish that her grandma was still alive? One last time Rebecca looked back at her parents, who were still speaking with the funeral director. She breathed a sigh, half of relief and half of resignation, and looked back to Nanna, still lying in the coffin…and staring back at her with eyes wide open.

Rebecca's heart skipped a beat and she nearly broke into a coughing fit she gasped so hard. She took a step back, her hands pressed to her chest so tightly that it started to hurt.

"Please, Rebecca," her grandmother said, continuing to lie in the casket, unwilling or unable to sit up. Rebecca squeezed her interlaced fingers to the point her fingers turned purple. "Come here a moment. I have a favor to ask of you."

The edge of the casket kept Rebecca from a view of her supposedly deceased grandmother. Standing on tiptoes from where she stood, she could just make out to tip of Nanna's nose.

"Please, Becca," Nanna pleaded in a soft, quavering voice. Her grandmother was the only one who ever called her "Becca" besides her Aunt Jessica.

Strangely, the fear she felt melted away after hearing this. It was clear to her that this had to be her grandmother, no demon from Hell or evil spirit. Rebecca didn't look back to her parents this time. She felt a pulling in her chest, like someone had hooked her with a fishing line and was reeling her in, minus the pain of the hook actually puncturing her flesh.

Her small steps took her to the edge of the platform on which the wooden sarcophagus sat. She locked eyes with her grandmother, who flashed a warm smile at her.

"Darling Becca," she whispered. "I will miss you, sweetheart."

Tears began to well up in Rebecca's young eyes. She wiped them away with the hem of her "Sunday's-best" dress.

"Now, about that favor," her grandmother said.

"Anything, Nanna."

"I need you to taste me," Nanna said.

"Rebecca didn't reply. She thought for sure that she had misunderstood what her grandmother had said.

"Um, did you say you want me to *take* you somewhere?" she asked.

"No," her grandmother replied, "I said I want you to *taste* me."

Again, Rebecca was stunned at the request and her silence made it apparent.

"My finger would be fine," Nanna assured her. "The little one, if you prefer." Again, she gave Rebecca a kind smile that reached her eyes.

Never one to disobey her grandmother, and afraid to disregard what was most assuredly her final wish, she replied, "OK, but just a taste."

Rebecca reached into the casket, grabbed her grandmother's cold hand, and shoved her pinky finger into her mouth. Surprisingly, it didn't taste that bad and deep in her mind, she felt satisfied with the good deed she'd done.

"Rebecca!" she heard her name shrieked from behind her. She turned to around to see who the voice belonged to, the graying digit still between her lips. Her Aunt Jessica must have just arrived. "What the hell are you doing?"

She looked from her aunt, over to where her parents and Mr. Smith/Schmidt stood (all three wearing shocked looks on their faces), back to her grandmother, who was lying in her casket, quiet, still and very much dead.

"Bud she ast me du daste her," she managed from around Nanna's pinky.

"Take that out of your mouth!" her father shouted, stomping over to her. She did as she was told and dropped the hand back on top the corpse.

That was the first time Rebecca had tasted a dead body, but it wouldn't be her last. After that day, dead things just started talking to her, and they also asked from the same thing.

"Taste me, please?"

And as much as her parents and her aunt and pretty much every other person who had ever come across her doing so told her just how wrong it was to taste road kill, or a dead pet goldfish, or a dearly departed relative, she just couldn't help it.

Her Aunt Jessica had taken her to a psychiatrist, or psychologist, (Rebecca never really understood the difference) without her parents' permission, any type of "doctory" practice being against their religion. Aunt Jessica, however, had no qualms about trying to get her niece some help.

The appointment went pretty well, Rebecca's aunt sitting in to listen, but not interrupting. She simply let the doctor talk to Rebecca and make his diagnosis. After the session was over, the two adults stood up from their comfy chairs.

"Rebecca," the doctor said, "your aunt and I are going to step outside of the office for just a second. We're going to talk a few things over. Are you going to be alright in here?"

She didn't reply for a few moments, seemingly staring off into space.

"I think I'll be fine," she finally said, not taking her eyes from the trophy fish mounted above the doctor's desk.

The two adults glanced at each other, and then back at Rebecca, sharing a slightly concerned look between them before leaving through the office door and shutting it gently. Rebecca stood up from her chair.

Outside the office…

"I've never really seen anything like this," the doctor said to Jessica.

"What do you mean by that?" she asked incredulously. "I mean, you are a professional, right? In all the years you've been doing this, in all the patients you've seen, you can't possibly tell me that Becca is the worst case you've had."

He raised his hands defensively, trying to calm her.

"Now, I never said she was the worst case I'd had," he said in an attempt to placate Jessica. "I simply said that I, personally, have never encountered anything like what your niece has."

"Well, what's wrong with her?" Jessica crossed her arms, waiting for an explanation.

"To start with, it appears that she has Asperger's Syndrome. From what you're telling me about her parents, it's not surprising that she was never diagnosed earlier. Our conversation today, along with what you've told me of the trouble she has with even the simplest social interactions, makes me fairly confidant in that conclusion, although more screening should be done. Also…"

Jessica continued listening, a sinking feeling spreading in her gut. With no children of her own, Becca has always been like a surrogate daughter to her. She took every chance to spend time with her, especially after her brother's religious conversion and joining the cult of Christian Science. He constantly tried to shove his religious rhetoric down her throat. She didn't see it as healthy for Becca, and with what she was hearing, it was worse than she'd thought.

"… she seems to be suffering from some sort of schizophrenia, but…" he paused, trying to find the right way to explain it" … well, normally, a schizophrenic person *hears* voices, but from what Becca says, these dead people and animals talk to her and she actually *sees* it, too."

"So, what's the difference?" Jessica asked.

"Well, it may not seem like much, it's just another thing I'll need to look into." He continued, "Now, these dead things are telling her to… taste them. Here's the third thing we're looking at. The symptoms seem to be pointing to an *OCD* that causes her to feel that she needs to taste every dead thing she comes across."

Jessica waited for more bad news from the good doctor, but he seemed to be done. She wiped at the tears that were forming in her eyes.

"Wha…" She cleared her throat as she choked on the word. "What can we do for her?"

"That depends," the doctor said. "Her parents' beliefs are going to prevent us from doing much of anything."

"Let's pretend that they aren't part of the picture."

He didn't say anything at first, looking down at the floor and picking at one finger with another.

"Look, Jessica. I could get in trouble for just seeing her today, but you're a friend, so I agreed to it."

"And I appreciate it."

"Great," he said. "But I could get a huge fine if Rebecca's parents were to find out about this and decided to pursue legal action. I could even lose my license."

"Alan, please," she begged. "What can we do to help her? What if I were to sue for custody? I mean, what they're doing; it's got to be something like… neglect or something, right? You could recommend that she be given treatment, and I know my brother. He'll start talking crazy about praying and Jesus healing her. They'll have to take her away from them."

Again, he looked down at the floor, contemplating.

"There are some drugs we could give her to stem the auditory and visual hallucinations. Therapy and counseling… it's going to be lots of work, Jessica. And that's only if you get custody."

The look he received from the determined woman left no question that she was not afraid of the fight ahead of them all.

"Right, then," he said. "Well, let's get back in there and she how Rebecca is doing."

The doctor opened the door to his office and acted the gentleman, holding it open for Jessica. She was greeted with a disturbing sight and let out a choked squeak as the doctor walked into the room.

"Um, Rebecca, my dear," he said, "it's not polite to lick another person's fish."

Aunt Jessica had won custody of her. Over the years, she had limited contact with her mother and virtually no contact with her father. Even at such a young age, the Church of Christian Science had felt it necessary to make a huge production of her excommunication. Her father refused chancing that they might do the same to him should he cavort with the heretic.

Her aunt put her through college. Rebecca had started medical school, but halfway through her second year, she had run out of her medication and had been so busy with studying and homework that she'd forgotten to refill the prescription. She'd been expelled when she'd been caught licking the training cadavers.

That's when she'd decided to take a job as a mortician. The hours were set to where she could be alone, and what was the worst that could happen should she miss her medication again? At least she'd have plenty of company...

Several decades later, after the custody battle between her aunt and her parents, after years of therapy and drugs and love from Aunt Jessica, after school and college, she found herself again standing over a dead body, waiting for it to ask her for a favor.

She hadn't worried about such things for some time. The medications she took every morning had kept the dead at bay for several years. Today, however, had thrown everything off. The power in her apartment building had gone out, causing her alarm to not go off. She slept during the day, so when she finally woke up at 9:37 PM, she only had twenty-three minutes to get across town to work.

At that point, her OCD kicked in and, her routine already thrown off, she had a small but intense panic attack, threw on some clothes, and left her apartment without taking her meds.

So she waited… but not for long.

His eyes popped open and he looked around at his surroundings before his eyes rested on Rebecca. He gave her a nervous but somehow hopeful smile. He was only slightly less good-looking than she suspected he had been in life. She couldn't help but smile back shyly.

He opened his mouth, but before he could speak…

"I know what you're going to ask," Rebecca said.

He cocked an eyebrow.

"You do, do you?"

"Yes," she replied, "and you're crazy if you think I'm going to do it."

"I'm crazy," he chuckled. "Little lady, you're the one here having a conversation with a dead guy and you think I'm the crazy one?"

"You know what I mean," she huffed. "I'm just off my meds. You're not even really talking. You're just a figment of my imagination. A part of my disease."

"Now hold on," he protested. "That's hurtful talk."

He turned his head away slightly. She could hear the popping of tendons and muscles that had tightened up. She looked down at his once dark brown eyes, which had by now filmed over. They did look genuinely hurt though.

"I... I'm sorry," Rebecca said. "I didn't mean to hurt your feelings. It's just..."

"That's alright," he said, turning fully back towards her, his charming, dead smile back in place. "You can make it up to me."

Rebecca rolled her eyes. She knew what was coming... or so she thought.

"I was murdered," he said. He lies still and silent in anticipation of a response. None came for a time. "Did you hear me?"

"I, uh, wait, what?" Rebecca said.

"I was listening to the coroner talking when he was working me over. He said that cause of death accidental," the corpse said. "It wasn't. You're the only one who can stop the murderer from getting away with it."

"But, I, well..." Rebecca said. "Don't you want me to taste you?"

The dead man didn't reply at first, but gave her a rather incredulous look for a stiff.

"Why on earth would I want you to taste me?" he asked.

"Everybody does," she said. "That is, all of the dead people and animals and such." She shrugged. "It's kind of my thing, I suppose."

"I just told you that I was murdered, and you want to taste me?" he said. "Maybe you are crazy."

"Well, duh!" she said. "Look, you want me to help you catch your killer, and after all these years... I mean, the drugs help, and... the sessions, but... I'm just feeling a little compelled so if I could just..."

After all of the years of being "normal" Rebecca realized that she missed the taste. It was part of her and she wanted it as much as the dead that asked her to taste them did.

Rebecca grabbed his graying toe and wiggled it playfully. A rather disgusted look crossed his face.

"I mean, I did just wash you, so I know you're clean," she said. "Then I promise I'll help you."

"Fine," he said, turning his head away. "But just a taste."

THE UNTOLD STORY OF HARVEY BARNES
BY D.G. SUTTER

The family business was looking after the dead, it had been for generations. For Harvey it was not a profession to look forward to, he was squeamish and feared death. Unfortunately the day was inevitable when his father would die, and when it came, Harvey was quick to the tavern.

His father Matthew was a well-respected Puritan man, and a paramount citizen. He had come to Salem straight from England. Harvey had no memory of the homeland, for his existence was lived almost entirely in the fishing village. It was a small commune, and death was infrequent. Sufficed to say, they lived poorly.

It was easier for Harvey to get by with a friend like George. Money fell from the Cornell family tree, practically a disposable commodity, and George wound up covering Harvey's bill most of the time. George attended to the bar hand.

"Excuse me, mum?"

The busty woman behind the counter turned. She wore a black bodice over a red dress. Her hair was done up in a spider's web. "Can I get you something?"

George held two fingers. "Two more malts."

She looked scornfully back over her shoulder. "I didn't hear no please."

"I hadn't said one."

The woman grudgingly fixed two brews, making it a point to pour them slowly. George tapped his fingers in a row. "She's really doing this all to bother me, you know."

"When in the world were women allowed to work the bar?" Harvey asked.

George let out a short fizz of air to let Harvey know that he didn't particularly care for the idea either. "She owns the place. I heard she murdered her husband to get at it."

Then he leaned in real close, so close that Harvey could taste the beer on his breath. "I heard she's a witch."

Harvey laughed at the preposition. He searched George's eyes for a hint of jest, but his brows stuck in a serious spot like two statues.

"C'mon George, you don't really believe that fodder," Harvey said sipping his glass.

"Supposedly keeps little felt dolls in her cellar. She pushes pins into em', like they's real people. Some sort of negro magic."

George regarded the woman again. She hunched in the dark corner rubbing her long fingers through her brown curls. Harvey rather liked the look of her, could even see himself bedding her.

"Look how she's clothed," George said with the curl of a distasteful lip. "She's want for a dirty tumble." He snickered a vile laugh and slammed his glass down on the wooden counter, not before stomaching the liquid.

"*Bridget!*"

She raised her head and ceased the brushing of her locks. They weren't the only three in the tavern and the way George had shouted attracted the attention of the other two gentlemen relaxing in the corner. One wore a fluffy grey beard and matching eyebrows, the other had a full moon face, pale as the surface.

"Why don't you fetch me another brew, you *wench*?"

Bridget's face changed from curious to furious in a blink, and her face grew pink as a rose. George slid his glass across the counter until it slammed on its side at the far end.

"George," Harvey pleaded, "leave her be. You're drunk." He grabbed onto George's shoulder lightly, but George shrugged it off aggressively.

"And clean that up while you're at it!"

George cackled beyond control. It was too dramatic and a tad maniacal. The scene embarrassed Harvey. He wanted to tell Bridget that he could protect her, that George was a donkey's behind. Bridget got to wiping up the mess with a brown rag. When done, she hid George's glass under the bar.

"Where's my beer, tramp?" He laughed that awful laugh again, amusing only himself by his debauchery. Harvey could see the hole in his smile, one which had never bothered him before, but all of a sudden made him want to shove something sharp through the gap.

Bridget didn't respond. Harvey looked at George smiling demonically and lost recognition of his friend. "George I think it's about time you left," he said.

He turned and stared at Harvey incredulous. "Is that the respect I get? For paying your tab?"

It was an honest response. Harvey could tell it wasn't the alcohol speaking, but something that surfaced as a result of the booze, some hidden grudge George held against him.

"You know what—"George dug into his vest pocket and pulled out a handful of coin. He tossed it onto the counter and it splayed across the floor with a clanging. "Pay your own damn way."

With that he left the tavern. Harvey wouldn't see him in a good number of years, and under a far different set of circumstances.

Bridget poured a cup of steaming tea for Harvey, who sat at the table with his ankle crossed over his left knee. His britches rode up just enough for his socks to voice protest against the chill air of November. She placed the kettle onto the stove top, where it whistled and smoked. Then, she sat diagonally from Harvey, the seat in which she always rested.

"How long have we been seeing one another now?" He asked.

Bridget frowned, which he had not expected. She was

supposed to be pleased with their stint, even disappointed that she hadn't met him sooner. "Three months or so, I would say."

Harvey smiled into her face and reached across the table for her light pink hand, dusted in powder. He cupped it in his palm, covered with dirt from the cemetery, the dead flesh crawling under his fingernails. "You know I absolutely adore you, don't you?"

Her hand went clammy inside his own, and slowly retracted into her lap, meeting the other, whilst her head tilted downward in shame.

"What's the matter, dear?" He asked concerned.

"There's a thing I've been keeping from you."

Harvey swallowed and it pained him. *What could she be hiding?* He was prepared to lay his love on the line, and she was keeping secrets?

"Get on with it."

"I'm married."

Harvey stood feeling dizzy. He paced about in front of the table with his hand on his forehead. "How?"

"James has been away to England on business. I haven't told a soul about our affair."

Harvey hadn't either, but that didn't mean it wasn't cherished. "What about us, Bridget? Will you claim it all a farce? Surely, there were true feelings involved."

"There were--I mean, there are--but — "

"Then nothing. How can you deny me?"

"James returns next week."

Harvey's anger rose to a point where he nearly backhanded her. George had been right all those months ago, he thought. Her *flashy* dress branded her a no good whore. The door slammed closed behind him. He was a fool not to realize before then, why she never let him use the front.

Twenty years passed and Harvey's business truly started to thrive. As folk immigrated to Salem and the Northern coast, he cashed in on the deprivation of others. There were few undertakers in the area, and his prices were more modest. Sometimes he traveled into the great city of Boston, all a bustle with the British army and import ships.

He never married nor had a subsequent affair, and continued to spend his days and nights in pubs and taverns. He steered clear of Bridget's, though he thought of her daily. She was the one who got away, or the one he left behind. Losing her was the most unfortunate event in all his life, and it resulted in the seclusion of his personality and the recluse of his relationships. He became an introvert, conversing only with those he was forced to, families of the deceased and market owners.

He was in the quarters his father had built, surrounded by grey bricks and the smell of stale death, preparing the body of the honorable judge Richard Hathorne. The man's skin was wrinkly and flaked. Harvey applied lotion, which was wrested from whale's blubber, to moisturize. Once it dried he proceeded to apply make-up.

Richard Hathorne had been appointed by the King himself. He was known for his merciful rulings and rotund stomach. In Harvey's days of socialization he had rather enjoyed the judges company. A large turnout was inevitable for such a man of repute, and the face would need to be beautiful.

In the middle of the make-up application, however, there came a purposeful knock upon the door. Harvey tossed the gloves onto the side table adjacent to the frame, coated in corpse juice, and swung wide the door. Beyond the threshold was a face twenty years older. It was topped with a set of grey hairs, but he could never forget those brown eyes flecked with bright orange shapes. The visitor tipped his tri-cornered hat down in salutation.

"Afternoon, Mr. Barnes."

Harvey felt his throat constrict. He couldn't speak, there was a frog in his throat which was not eager to leap, but he cleared it with a gulp. "George." He nodded. "What do you want?"

"After all these years," George said, shaking his solemnly. "You're still trying to keep me in place."

Harvey squinted at the man, his old friend, come knocking on his door after all the years. Since the souring of their friendship, George had gone on to become the Sheriff. He assumed it was an unhealthy purpose that delivered George to his doorstep.

"I came to ask of you a favor."

Harvey glared skeptically. What had suddenly possessed George to seek out his assistance? And seeing as his business was the dead, what had George done?

"What sort of rut have you gotten yourself stuck in?"

"Try not to dismiss too quickly. You do this for me, you'll be rewarded handsomely."

"Go on."

"There's been a murder. Sam Powell."

Harvey knew of Sam Powell, but didn't *know* Sam Powell. He owned the corn field just over the hill from the cemetery. Why anyone would want to kill the elderly man was beyond Harvey's comprehension. "So you would like me to fix the body?"

"I would. But that's not what I've come for. Seeing as you're the local undertaker, I was wonderin' if you'd be the hangman."

"I think it's about time you left."

Harvey started to close the door, but Georges strong hand pulled it back open.

"Same old line, huh Harvey?"

Harvey fiddled with his apron uncomfortably. "I'm not going to hash out the past with you."

"Then live in the present. You deal with the dead.

Nobody else has got the stomach for the job. It's yours to take or leave."

Harvey wasn't impressed with the job offer. He didn't want to be considered a killer. "Do I get a mask?"

George chuckled that sick laugh, the one from the bar. It made Harvey's stomach tickle. "You can wear whatever you damn please as long as you pull that rope. After you see the body, you'll be glad to hang the bastard."

The wooden coffin of oak was lowered into the ground. There was a small ceremony for Mr. Powell, while Sheriff George Cornell cleared out the house and burned the structure to the ground, claiming evil spirits would gather there. Harvey remembered the superstitious side of George, making Harvey skip the cracks else wise break his mother's back, claiming broken mirrors were worth seven years of bad luck, and it seemed they were only getting stranger.

Harvey pulled the black felt mask over his head and straddled his horse, Jessie. It was a cold night for a hanging. The last he could remember was when he was just a boy. The criminal had raped a woman, and he was sentenced to hang by the neck. The politics in Salem had changed, become a bit more---Democratic---but Harvey knew little of the politics in town. He rarely dealt with people, unless forced, and even then in short offerings.

They were to meet across from the Meeting House and proceed out of town, just South of Danvers. Once at the river the business would begin. Harvey held the reigns with his left and a lantern with his right. Somewhere in the woods a barn owl hooted, a deep cooing sound. The path curved through a canopy of dead trees with brown leaves. Wings fluttered in the branches, twigs snapped, and Harvey clutched the reigns tight in fear.

Outside the Meeting House were gathered five men on horseback and a shackled individual in tattered white rags, who was surprisingly young. George held the rope which tied between the shackles.

"Let's ride," he said.

The ride was pleasurable despite the knowledge of a despicable task ahead. They traveled until they reached the outer bounds, and the dead town of Danvers could be seen across the murky North River. There was the smell on the air of moisture, like a winter come too early for all, which would blanket the Earth leaving death in its wake. No souls were around, at least none Harvey could see. He could tell George wanted the act forgotten.

As they strode onto the summit of the hill, Harvey could see a whimsical tree. From it hung a thirteen knot noose. The wind was strong enough to tremble the taut rope and Harvey could feel it blistering his cheeks, reddening them to the point of stinging.

George hopped from his horse and started to untie the captive. "Try any nonsense, and you'll be hacked to bits."

The shackles were left on the wrists as Harvey led the man up the stairs of the wooden platform. The prisoner tried to glimpse into the eyeholes of the mask, but Harvey wouldn't allow for it. He also whispered to himself, swift and inaudible words. His voice sounded like a snakes slither.

Harvey lassoed the man's neck in the noose and walked down the stairs. The criminal did not weep or plead, or beg, but took his punishment as a man. Something about his collectiveness worried Harvey.

George said, "For the murder of Samuel Flynn Powell, thou art sentenced to be hung by the neck! May the good Lord have mercy upon your soul! Have you any last words?"

"You have all sinned in the name of Lucifer, his children are protected. Thou art destined to a life of servitude in his name and punishment shall be due given--in the form of eternal curse--to you, against your children--"

George nodded and Harvey pulled the rope to remove the platform on which the man stood. There was a loud crack, his feet twitched and the body began to spin in circles. The tongue popped out of the corpse's mouth, and onto the ground. Blood oozed greedily from the mouth.

"Take care of it," George stated matter-of-factly.

Harvey's words caught in his throat as George and his gang rode off into the night. The body was still warm when Harvey untied it, something he never felt.

Rumors spread around Salem, of witchcraft and sorcery, of coming storms of magical depravity. Children started to claim possessions and haunting in the middle of the night. Harvey continued to stray from the workings of the town as much as possible, but it was almost impossible to ignore the stirrings.

He felt it had much to do with the hanging of the man the previous winter. Not a night went by he didn't think of that sickening crack. When preparing the dead, he pictured bruises circling their necks, blood drizzling out of the lips. The bodies would animate in his mind, reach for him. He knew they were hallucinations, but they hindered his abilities.

The grave he had buried the man in was shallow and rested next to the North River. Sometimes he would visit the site, unmarked and unknown to the world. He hadn't even known the man's name. Every so often he placed a bouquet on the spot, only to find them withered and abandoned on the next trip.

Thus, he rendered it an awful omen when a knock of similar character came upon the door of the preparation room. Harvey paced to the entrance and eased it open. George looked deranged and drunk. His hair was a mess and his eyes bounced about inside his head. The man had really gone off the deep end. He'd heard stories about the Sheriff from "customers". That he was jailing "witches", and even pressed one man to death with stones for not admitting his guilt in sorcery.

"Harvey, Harvey, Harvey."

"George."

He burped then, and Harvey was hit with a gust of whiskey. "I need your help--with an infraction."

"George, I--"

The sheriff straightened his somber jacket and closed one eye. "Are you refusing to cooperate?"

George was on a power trip. Resisting would do no good, for George would find a way to incriminate him. Harvey was under the thumb of the most powerful man in Salem. It would be to his benefit to attend to the task and be on with his life.

"No, it's just I have a body to get ready."

"Well ice it, it ain't getting any deader. I need you for another hanging."

"String it up!" George shouted.

There was a much larger crowd, near thirty people. Harvey had ridden on his own. George had the nerve to ask if he recalled the place. Not only did he recall, he dreamt of it every time he closed his eyes, in a nightmarish way.

"We're here today, for the first, of many of a coven of filthy, dirty witches, has admitted to the craft of the *devil!* I would suggest all watching, carry this as an example! Bring her forth!"

From the back of the crowd the Sheriff's cronies forced the woman forward. Her head was wrapped in black linen much like Harvey's hangman mask, except there were no eyeholes. She protested, shrieking and flailing her arms, kicking her legs, trying to break loose. They dragged her up the wooden steps, and Harvey noticed the age of her body. She had veiny legs and wrinkly grey skin. It was an older woman.

"Avert your eyes, or fall under her curse!" George said.

The hood was torn from her head and Harvey recognized the face of Bridget instantly. Her hair had gone pure white, but her beauty remained unadulterated. Tears walked down her cheeks.

"I han't done a thing! By the word of the good Lord, I'm innocent I tell you!"

Harvey placed the loop over her neck. She had rejected him. She was a witch and a liar. Once she had shown him her basement collection of stored potions, spices, and magical items.

George said, "Here in our home, a demon hath breached. May she be delivered to hell with haste, and lighten our lives of this burden!"

"You're the ones who'll BURN IN HELL. YOUR CHILDREN MAY AS WELL BE BORN UNDER A BAD SIGN." Her voice lowered then, as her eyes locked on Harvey's eyeholes, so that he and only he could hear.

"I know those eyes Mr. Hangman. Don't you worry your little heart; there'll be no happy ending for any of us."

George screamed, "LET THE WITCH HANG!"

The crowd erupted as the floor fell out. Harvey didn't hear a snap, but heard a sound like a bit of air escaping from someone's mouth. The flesh on his arms rose and the back of his throat tickled. He made the mistake of looking into her accusing eyes.

Harvey could prepare no more bodies. Each time he looked at the eyes, incantations filled his head, whispers off the walls. Cabinets were flipped open, and windows tinkered though nothing was tapping, as if something was trying to enter. No longer could he visit the spot where the bodies were buried, up on Gallow's Hill. Branches crunched on the ground, like surrounding footsteps. Yells came in the air though no one was present. However, the draw to it was undeniable.

He walked through the town on foot, as he'd been doing so often at night. Through the walls of the houses voices spoke to him. They told him names, names of the guilty. "Scream them out," the voices would say, "Tell all the world of these evils."

Harvey had secretly been telling two young girls through their window. He would creep to it and fog it with his breath, then scribble the names with his finger. They were townsfolk, women, most of them old; but Bridget insisted they were witches. He felt the need to tell someone. The girls cowered and cried, telling him to leave them be.

Then one night, he returned to Gallow's Hill. There, overlooking Danvers, a platform was erected. The voices picked up and the branches cracked, leaves swirled about. A group surrounded him.

"You've been fiddling with witchery Harvey."

Harvey stood over Bridget's grave. "I swear I han't. These voices have been speaking to me."

"It's the voice of the dark lord. He's invaded you." George said.

"I'm a Christian man, George…You know it."

They grabbed at him, but Harvey backed away. He nearly slipped into the North River. Two of the men in black masks finally accosted him. A noose was thrown around his neck. George dragged him up the stairs by the other end, choking him.

"You'll sleep with the Devil tonight."

Those were the last words Harvey Barnes heard before his neck broke. He never knew it would end that way, at least his first life. They say if you walk about Salem at night, real late, one can still hear the footsteps of Harvey Barnes, cracking branches and fogging windows on his way, searching for retribution.

ONE NIGHT IN DETROIT
BY DC SCHAROUN

"Great!" I exclaim to no one in particular. "Another long, boring night pulling the graveyard shift."

It had been a very hot and wet summer, and tonight was no different. It's one of those nights where there's zero air movement and the humidity is in the high 90's. The hot, wet air condenses on my skin and mixes with the streams of sweat pouring out of my body. Niagara Falls has less water than my forehead. Downstairs is hotter still. The air in the basement is dead. Hell feels colder. The tall, grey concrete walls have no windows and no fans, but the residents never complain. Their stay is short enough anyway.

Perhaps I should have worn my bathing suit tonight.

I'm two months into my residency at a temporary morgue in Detroit, Michigan after having received an AOS in Mortuary Sciences at Simmonds Institute in Syracuse, New York. I work with the records of the deceased, checking official autopsy reports, filling out death certificates and matching the body bags that keep coming in from a very busy summer due to an outbreak of violent murders. The mayor has imposed a dusk-to-dawn curfew and called in the National Guard to restore order.

All that and I'm working alone tonight! My two co-workers called in sick. Only one of them is actually sick. The other is just a tool. He wants to go to a party or a rave or whatever they call it these days. Why is it when there's a curfew everyone wants to go somewhere all of a sudden? Well, somewhere except work.

The Guard stopped and questioned me four times on the way in to work. Eventually, they let me through; my work is considered vital to processing for the City of Detroit. The Angel of Death has been camping over the city for months now, with no end in sight.

The facilities that I'm currently working in were quickly converted into a temporary morgue from a bomb shelter that was built in the early 1950's. The tools and equipment in the morgue are also from the 1950's. No state of the art fridges here. Nothing but old appliances that the Department of Health may as well have scrounged up from the dump.

The freezers have to be checked with a thermometer every half hour to make sure the residents stay cool. Frequent power outages have occurred over the past few days. There are twelve chest freezers total, all with rusty hinges and latches. Three are currently occupied with nine on standby, as a precautionary measure. The only light that shines bleakly in the room is from one overhead fluorescent bulb with no cover. The light casts a pale, spectral glow across the scattered records sprawling over the table top, forcing the autoclave in the corner to surrender to the shadows around it.

I glance at the clock and grunt in disgust. 2:15 AM. The shift started at 10:30PM. It's time to take a break to escape this oppressive tomb. Checking the temperatures of the three occupied freezers, two of the freezers are well within range while the third is barely in the zone. Thirty nine degrees. Above forty and there would be problems, which means more paperwork to fill out. But for now the residents inside are fine, zipped up tight and tidy in their black bedcovers.

I hastily scribble down the temperatures on my nightly report. I don't care about spelling or legibility; the records can be fudged later if need be. Drooling in anticipation of the upcoming break, I carelessly shut the door on the third freezer and hurry through the rest of my checks. I want to take the full half-hour to thoroughly enjoy the next task before me this evening...

Removing the small round key that sits in the top desk drawer, I cross to the cabinet marked "Flammables." The key trembles ever so slightly in my fingers in sweet anticipation. I swear under my breath; the key is *not* sliding as smoothly as it normally does in the lock. The key drops on the floor and I curse loudly. It doesn't really matter though, as cursing falls on dead ears.

As I pick up the key, sweat drips off my hand creating a tiny pool on the floor. A mad gleam is starting to grow, coming from the back of my eyes, as the key successfully slides home in the lock. Sweat tastes salty and bitter as it slides down my forehead and across my lips. I reach in for the bottle labeled *Formaldehyde* and draw it slowly towards me. It is a most treasured prize!

Locking the cabinet now would be pointless. Rather the doors are left to creak open. Records are shuffled aside to uncover the small 500 milliliter beaker that resides permanently on the desk. Gently, ever so gently, the deadly nectar is poured into the beaker till it is half -full. Anxious, I set the remainder of the formaldehyde on the floor next to the desk.

Next, three cigarettes are rolled. After each one is packed and rolled tightly, they get a soaking in the formaldehyde. They only have to soak for a minute or two and then they're ready!

As I walk back up the thirteen steps to the entry door, I recall the first time I watered my cigarettes. It was back in school, to take the edge off the stress of classes and homework. Now it takes the edge off of working with the chilly residents below. There's a certain type of person that can handle the dead well, and with dignity. Look elsewhere for that person.

The back stoop is barely lit with the twin from the crypt downstairs; a single bulb hanging from a cord which continuously flickers. Bringing out a matchbook from my pocket, I light up and inhale deeply. My lungs catch on fire and burn as the acrid smoke pulls deep into them. I immediately feel the rush that the fluid gives it.

As the flame from the last cigarette dies out, Murphy's Law has decided to add yet another depressing element to this already oppressive, miserable night...the naked bulb guarding the back stoop goes out. I blink into the darkness for a few seconds before realizing that the bulb will not come back on its own. It is truly dead.

Funny how little you appreciate light until the absence of it. Despite drifting off on my high, something faintly clicks in the back of my brain. Not only did the single, naked bulb above me go out, but all of the lights around are out. It is pitch black, and overcast, and very, very dark.

My curses come out a bit stuttered and slurred at this point. Hindsight is 20/20. The flashlight should have made the trip up the stairs with me, but did not. The matchbook comes out of my pocket yet again, and my fingers fumble with the cover. There are two matches left. Match one gets ripped out and dropped in my haste; it disappears into time and space. Match two is torn out of its home, more cautiously than the first. Fingers flip the cover over, oh so gently, slowly, carefully and strike it. Nothing.

After trying five times, seven times, fourteen times...after about the twentieth time of trying to light that last match, the matchbook is launched from my fingers at a high rate of speed, out into the darkness.

I slowly feel for the door knob to enter the tomb once more, as there is still a job to do. The residents must be pacified, no matter the cost.

The switch at the top of the stairs is useless as the light at the bottom is also out. Descending back down the stairs should be an interesting task as there is no light whatsoever to see by.

My fingers grip the cool, wet, metal rail and guide me down the stairs, carefully placing one foot out in front of the other.

Halfway down the left heel misses and slips off the step. Faltering, my fingers slip off the rail and I slide down the remaining steps, landing hard on my tailbone first, then a split second later the back of the head. I see stars in the darkness as the pain shoots up my back and my head feels like it's ready to explode.

It's then that the noise is first heard. It's a muffled bump coming from somewhere downstairs. Once. Twice. And a third time.

"Hullo?" I call out as I try to shake the stars from my head. We are still alone, the residents and I, so why am I hearing the noise? A hallucination, perhaps?

"Hullo? Is anyone there?"

No one answers the challenge. The dead can't speak. Listening in the darkness for any sort of noise, I relax after a moment as my brain registers that I am alone.

Then three muffled thumps sound through the silence again.

I pull myself up slowly --- partially so I will not fall again and partially because I'm in agony from the fall. I'm lightheaded and dizzy. Nausea is working its way up my throat. I choke back the pain and the bile.

The rush from the laced cigarette has started to die away. The headache is getting worse by the second. Is my mind playing tricks on me? Did I really hear those muffled thumps?

Three more muffled thumps answer my unspoken questions. Louder this time and more insistent. The thumping may be coming from inside one of the freezers! In my drug-induce state I can't tell which one. Slowly, methodically and blindly, I work my way around the room, carefully feeling the walls. The heat and humidity are oppressive and stifling; I am suffocating.

THOOMP! THOOMP! THOOMP!

The banging in the room echoes the banging in my head. Reaching the first freezer, I slowly open the door and find it's as warm as the room-temperature.

"What the hell?"

Thankfully, this one is empty…

THOOMP! THOOMP! THOOMP!

The noise sounds like someone panicking, trying to escape. Short, ragged breaths are choking me. My chest is getting tight from the adrenaline rush of fear and pain.

My fear is that if this is a person that should not have been bagged they could run out of air. Death by suffocation is horrible if you are awake to experience it. First, there is panic as you're aware you are going to die. Then you pass out and never wake.

In my rush, my feet stumble and kick against a glass jar and it breaks, spilling the contents over the linoleum tiles.

"Shit," I mutter out of annoyance that I'll have to clean it up later. Then it hits me.

The formaldehyde!

Now the cursing is much more violent and continuous, until I'm rudely cut off...

THOOMP! THOOMP! THOOMP!

The banging sounds as if it's coming from the back freezer, closest to the back wall, where resident three lays waiting for me to attend to. Normally my brain would be completely freaking out of by now, telling me to run as far away as possible, but there's still a little numbness from my smoke left in me. I suddenly feel a desire to prove my six years of schooling wasn't for naught and an unusual duty to the dead. Or living, as this case very well may be.

My fingers find the handle of the freezer in question.

THOOMP! THOOMP! THOOMP!

I feel the vibration through the handle! The door opens and I find the temperature is still on the cool side. Colder than the other freezer I'd encountered, but the frost I expected to find on the inside door of an occupied freezer is merely condensation now. Not a good sign.

I reach in and feel around. The bag is there but the zipper appears to be partially open.

THOOMP!

I jump back as the bag had moved with that last sound. Slipping on the formaldehyde, thankfully I catch myself on the desk before I fall again.

There's a crackle above my head that turns into a steady hum as the fluorescent light flickers back to life…

THE MOANING DEAD
BY NICK MEDINA

Mrs. Price fell down an open sewer six days ago. She's stuck down there and she hasn't shut her mouth about it since. She's endlessly moaning and no one will help her find her way out.

Abby Gardener hasn't slept since Mrs. Price fell in the sewer. Her father, Joseph Gardener, was the one who lifted the heavy grate off the street and opened the sewer in the first place. He took all the grates off the manholes up and down the block. He said it would help in case *they* ever came after the Gardeners.

Abby turned seven two days before Mrs. Price fell in the sewer. It was the last time she had what could be considered a sufficient meal - some rice mixed with beans, a boiled potato and a piece of fish from the freezer. Now she was hungry and tired, sad and scared. She tried to go to sleep, but every time she closed her eyes all she could focus on was the sound coming out of Mrs. Price's rotten mouth, which made its way past Abby's bolted bedroom window. Even when she tried to cry herself to sleep, Mrs. Price's moaning won the war.

Abby wasn't always so hungry and tired and scared. There was a time when the infected as a whole existed solely as a scary suspicion to the Gardeners, an unthinkable threat like some horrible nightmare born of speculation and rumors spread by the media and gossiped about by the neighbor's on their front porch steps. Abby would never forget the day those revolting rumors became real life.

She'd been watching a cardinal hop about from branch to branch in the tree outside her second-story bedroom window for about twenty minutes when it happened. It was a rare site to see a cardinal in the city. It hopped from the tree to the sign jutting out from the side of the three-story brick building; a sign that read *Gardener's Funeral Home*. The cardinal had just taken flight from the sign when Joseph Gardener started screaming.

Abby had never heard her father scream like that before. His cries came all the way up from the basement; they hit her ears as though he were standing right next to her. She startled with surprise and raced down the stairs to the kitchen on her way to the basement to see what was wrong. But her mother, Helen Gardener, stopped her with firm grip that pulled Abby tight against her aproned torso.

"Don't," was all Helen said. Abby could feel her mother's quickening pulse through the apron.

"What's wrong with Daddy?" Abby asked.

"I don't know," her mother whispered.

They both stood there in the kitchen staring toward the door - the barrier between the living and the dead - that led down to the basement. Ten torturous seconds ticked by before the basement door burst open and Joseph staggered into the kitchen.

"Daddy!" Abby screamed.

"Joseph, what happened?" Helen wondered, trying to keep her voice calm for her daughter's sake.

"No one's allowed in the basement," he said. He threw the door shut and fell back against it panting. What he didn't tell his family was that the young man who had died in a motorcycle accident the day before, and who he was about to embalm, had come back to life on the embalming table.

The young man had come back to life just like the others reported about on the news; he'd come back to life with bloodshot eyes and a hunger for human flesh. The bereft biker was at that moment lurching about the basement in search of a beating heart to make a meal out of.

Joseph had been a funeral director for twelve years and in that time he had laid thousands of souls to rest. But until the day that the cardinal appeared outside Abby's window, he had never seen a body come back to life.

He installed a deadbolt on the basement door that night. It came with three keys, one of which he kept. He threw the other two away. When Joseph Gardener began his business - shortly after marrying Helen and when Abby was no more than a twinkle in his eye - he bought the three-story brick building in the city to house it and his forthcoming family. The basement held the morgue. The first floor served a dual purpose; half of it was designated for the chapels where the viewings were held and the other half had the family's kitchen and dining room. The upper floors provided the primary living space.

"Should we tell her?" Joseph asked his wife in a whisper.

"Tell me what?" Abby asked. She had been standing outside her parents' bedroom, not exactly eavesdropping, but not exactly ignoring them either.

"Come here, sweetie," her father said. He rubbed his worn face, which looked older to Abby than it had the day before.

Abby approached him slowly. She felt funny and a little sick to her stomach as he picked her up and put her on his lap. It was the same feeling she had when he broke the news to her that her grandmother was dead.

"Something strange is happening, honey," he said.

"I know," she squeaked.

He smiled at her. "You know what Daddy does for a living," he said, not really asking, but not really stating either.

She nodded.

"Sometimes they don't stay asleep," he explained.

"They don't?"

He shook his head, his face grim.

"You don't have to worry," Helen said. "Daddy is going to keep us safe."

"I know," she said again.

"Good," Joseph said through tight lips. "You're a good

girl. Now go play and don't worry about anything, okay?"

"Okay," she agreed.

Helen and Joseph kissed their daughter on the top of her head and smiled until she scampered out of the room in search of her velveteen rabbit.

"Are we going to make it?" Helen asked when Abby was gone, her smile fading from her troubled lips.

"We're going to be fine," Joseph said. He hoped that he was right.

The truth was that Joseph had a difficult decision to make. Funerals brought in a good amount of money, but now they weren't the somber events they once were. He either had to continue with his workload as usual, thereby putting his family's safety in jeopardy by bringing the dead - each one like a ticking time bomb - into the house, or he had to take a pay cut and figure out how to make ends meet without his usual cash flow. He opted for the latter. He couldn't in good conscience put his family at risk, or himself for that matter. After all, they depended on him to bring home the bacon. He decided that for his family's sake he would work only as necessary, just enough to pay the bills and to put food on the table.

It wasn't just the Gardener's that changed in those first few days. It seemed to Abby that the whole world had changed. She wasn't allowed outside anymore. School was out of the question. She couldn't even go out to the swing set in the backyard. She never saw the neighbors like she used to. She missed shouting good morning to Mrs. Price, the old lady who lived down the street with a Cocker Spaniel named Steven and who always had pieces of caramel in her pocket to share.

Helen kept the doors shut and locked. The windows were bolted and the drapes were drawn at all times. Joseph and Helen seldom spoke above whispers and when Abby tried to sing they shushed her.

People rarely came to the house. The phone rang

occasionally, but that was only because the dead had to be dealt with no matter how dangerous they might be. Joseph was the only one allowed to leave the funeral home. He'd set out early in the morning when the sun was above the horizon and he always came back before it started to sink. Helen and Abby never knew when or if he returned with a body of the recently deceased. But they did know when he returned with an old, single shot, .22 caliber rifle one day.

"A gun, Joseph?" Helen asked, her voice a shocked whisper, when she saw the rifle.

"They're saying a head shot's the most effective way to stop them," he explained.

Helen's eyes went wide. "You know I don't like guns….Do you even know how to shoot that thing?"

"I'll learn," was all he said as he unlocked the basement door and disappeared into the morgue.

Abby had never been fond of the basement. She'd only ventured down there a couple of times, and it was just in the last year that she discovered enough courage to be in the kitchen alone - during the day of course. It was the silence that scared her, the lack of life at the bottom of the stairs. When she saw her father descend into the darkness with the rifle in his hand she knew she'd never be alone in the kitchen again no matter what time of day. The image forced her to comprehend more completely than before. *Why should Daddy need a rifle?* She wondered. The dead were supposed to be still. And she wasn't supposed to be scared.

The basement door - tall, broad, painted brown with an old brass knob - gave her the shivers. It was an ugly thing that concealed something much uglier. She didn't like that door. It haunted her. When she had bad dreams - which happened quite frequently following the day she heard her father scream - they always had something to do with that door. Sometimes it would shake in its frame. Sometimes she would hear the loud, clomping footfalls of people who had died as they struggled up the stairs to jiggle the knob.

The door haunted her even now. It was like a living thing, a monster. It seemed to grow larger before her. It protruded from its frame. It wanted to unleash the ugliness it harbored upon her. Abby shuddered and looked away.

"Mama? What's Daddy doing with that gun?" she asked Helen.

"Daddy's keeping us safe," she answered with a lump in her throat. "Don't you worry your pretty, little head. Everything's going to be all right." She kissed Abby all over her forehead and on the tip of her nose. She wiped away a tear from her own eye before Abby could see it streaming down her cheek.

No more than a minute after going downstairs, Joseph came up again with the rifle in his hand.

"What's going on?" Helen asked.

"It's jammed," he grunted. He engaged the deadbolt and went to the back door that led out to the yard where he disappeared once again.

Helen tried to give Abby a reassuring smile, but the corners of her mouth couldn't quite get high enough to make the smile look genuine. Abby smiled back. She needed to reassure her mother just as much as her mother needed to reassure her.

"What should we have for dinner tonight?" Helen asked in a blatant attempt at creating a distraction.

"Pizza and salad."

Helen yanked open the freezer door. "It looks like you're in luck," she whispered. "Cheese or pepperoni?" Abby pointed to the pepperoni pizza in her mother's left hand. The frozen disk fell to the floor when a gunshot rang out from the backyard.

"Sounds like he fixed it," Helen said with a nervous chuckle. Tears glistened in the corners of her eyes. "Sorry, baby, but I don't think there'll be any salad to go with the pizza."

Dinner in the Gardener household wasn't the exquisite

affair it used to be. Like the pizza, Helen only had prepackaged foods to prepare. The vegetables were frozen instead of fresh. The meat came loaded with preservatives instead of coming straight from the butcher. But the Gardeners were among the lucky ones. At least they had food on the table and a roof over their heads. Some homes had been invaded. It hadn't happened in their neighborhood yet, but they knew it was happening nearby because they'd seen it on the news.

"What'd you do today, sweetie?" Joseph asked his daughter between bites of his pepperoni slice.

"Nothing," she said. "I drew a picture of the park."

"I bet it's beautiful. Can I see it?"

Abby nodded her head rapidly. She took a bite of pizza and took off for the stairs to get the drawing from her bedroom.

"Don't run with food in your mouth," Helen called after Abby, being as loud as her whisper would allow.

"She's handling this so well," Joseph said.

"How can she grow up in a world like this?"

Abby was back before Joseph could answer. She hopped into his lap and held her drawing up for him to see. There were shades of green in the grass and the trees. The sky was bright blue. The sun was a brilliant yellow.

"It's perfect," Joseph said. He couldn't bring himself to break her heart by telling her that the grass in the real park was splattered with blood and that the ice-cream man no longer pushed his cart up and down the brick-paved paths; he just staggered around now with red and purple chunks of rotting flesh clinging to his smock.

Tapping that sounded like the repetitious thud of knuckles scraping against wood forced Abby to put her picture down. She knew what the tapping meant. It was something else she heard in her nightmares. It came from behind the basement door.

"Excuse me," Joseph said. He wiped his mouth with his

napkin and lifted Abby off his lap.

"Joseph?" Helen said, but that's all she said.

He went into the kitchen from the dining room. He had left the rifle propped by the basement door. He picked it up before disengaging the deadbolt.

"Why don't we go upstairs?" Helen asked Abby. "We can put on a movie. Your choice."

Abby's eyes were wide and her lips were tight. Her face paled ever so slightly. She didn't say or do anything until the rifle discharged. That's when she started screaming.

Joseph found two notes tacked to the front door the following morning. They were from neighbors not just asking but demanding that he stop putting the safe-so-far neighborhood in danger by dealing with the dead. Joseph was already working at a bare minimum. Any less and his family would starve. He crumpled the notes, threw them aside and went down to the morgue to work on his latest customer, after all not all of the dead were coming back to life, just some of them.

Joseph worked with his rifle at his side. He'd never feared the dead before, but now he strapped the bodies down to the table and stood as far back as possible. As an undertaker, he had a responsibility to respect the dead, but how could he respect the dead when he knew they could come back at any second and disrespect him and his family? Every little sound he heard, every little speck of dust that floated past the corner of his eye, made him jump. He hated the dead, but the dead were all he knew. He had nothing to fall back on.

He finished with the sixty-six year-old man he was working on and used the pulley to hoist the stiff into its casket. He closed the lid, locked it and went up to the kitchen for lunch.

"We're all out of everything," Helen said when he got upstairs.

"Everything?" he echoed.

"There's some rice…some pasta and jerky, but the bread's moldy, the eggs are gone and the freezer's just about empty."

"I'll go," he said.

"I'm sorry."

"You have nothing to be sorry about."

Joseph strapped the rifle over his chest, kissed his wife goodbye and set out to provide for his family. Helen locked the door behind him. She put the deadbolt into place, engaged the security chain and propped a chair beneath the doorknob. She went back to the kitchen and filled a pot with water for pasta. She stood over it, watching the tiny bubbles at the bottom of the pot get larger as the pot got hotter. The steam from the water felt good on her face.

"Mama?" Abby whispered from the kitchen doorway.

"Yes, dear?"

"I'm hungry."

"I'm making lunch. And Daddy's getting us some food. Go upstairs and play quietly. I'll come get you when it's ready."

Abby agreed with a nod. She made her way upstairs with a book of her favorite fairytales tucked beneath her arm.

The bubbles departed from the bottom of the pot. They floated to the top of the water where they gradually started a rolling boil. Helen picked up the one box of pasta she had left. She couldn't be sure over the rattle of the hard noodles inside the box, but she thought she heard a thunk. She paused, holding the box in her hand, waited and then poured when she didn't hear anything else. She stirred the noodles, subconsciously listening for sounds that she shouldn't be hearing over the gurgling boil. She glanced at the basement door. It was giving her an eerie sensation inside. Her gut told her something was wrong, but her mind told her she was letting her fear get the best of her.

She went on stirring, checking over her shoulder every few seconds. It was when she fished a noodle out of the pot to test its tenderness that the door frame behind her splintered and the lock gave way.

Helen screamed. She reacted to the dead man in her kitchen by heaving the pot off the stove and pouring the boiling hot water over the old man's head. The infected groaned, seemingly unaffected by the scalding shower Helen had given him, although his rotting and made-up flesh blistered and burned. He reached for Helen. She tried to run, but she slipped in the puddle on her kitchen floor. He caught her in his grasps.

"No!" she shrieked. "Please, no!"

Whether he understood her or not didn't make one bit of difference. He sunk his nails in her arms and then sunk his teeth in her throat. He gnashed and groaned until Helen had a gaping wound where her throat used to be. Soon she was staggering around the kitchen just like him.

Abby heard her mother's pleas for mercy all the way up in her room, but, whether out of denial or self-preservation, she didn't race down the stairs to see if she could help. She closed her bedroom door and went on reading until she heard the gunshots of her panicked father as he tried to get back inside the house.

"Oh my god!" Abby heard him scream when he got through the reinforced door. "Helen!"

The words were followed by two more gunshots and then his powerful footsteps as he pounded up the stairs.

"Abby," he gasped, his entire body melting into a heap of relief on his daughter's bedroom floor.

She closed the book. She knew what her father's tears meant. She knew that nothing would ever be the same ever again.

Abby stopped talking after the death of her mother. She wouldn't go into the kitchen; she wouldn't go downstairs at all for that matter. Joseph blamed himself for Helen's death. If only he had left her with the rifle. If only he had given up dealing with the dead when his neighbors told him to. If it weren't for Abby he would have given up on life, but having to care for her kept him sane even though he feared she had gone insane herself.

She hardly ate. She hardly slept. She spent most of her days sitting beside her bed, sometimes rocking in place, sometimes staring at the wall.

"Abby," Joseph said almost a month to the day after Helen had become one of the moaning dead, "it's your birthday." He did his best to make it special even though she didn't seem to notice. He cooked her dinner - giving her the last piece of fish they had left in the freezer - and brushed her hair while she eyed the wall. If they had flour and chocolate and eggs he would have attempted a cake, but they didn't have any of those things.

"I have to find us some more food," he said the next day. He had put it off for so long that they were now worse off than they were when Helen died. "If I don't go we'll starve," he tried to explain, hoping to get some sign of approval or understanding out of Abby.

"I'll be back," he said, his voice cracking. "I promise to come back." He got up and kissed his daughter. She blinked in response. He lifted the rifle from over his shoulder and placed it on her bed. It was ready to fire. "I'm leaving this with you," he said. "Just aim and pull the trigger."

Abby rocked some more.

"I love you, Abby." Joseph choked back the lump in his throat. He left his daughter not knowing if he'd ever see her again.

Abby used to be afraid of the silence produced by the dead. But now she was afraid of the noise that they made. At least the quiet ones couldn't hurt her. She hadn't seen her father in days, not since he left to find more food. She knew what that meant.

She stood up and staggered to the window in her bedroom where she pushed the curtains aside and looked at the world she hadn't seen since the day the cardinal was in the tree outside. The tree was still there. Its branches were bare. The street was empty. Her father was nowhere in sight. She could see the sewer that Mrs. Price - or the thing that used to be Mrs. Price - had fallen into. She couldn't see Mrs. Price, but she knew Mrs. Price was still stuck in the shaft because of the frightful noise that floated out of the sewer and onto the air. Abby pushed her hands hard against her ears. No matter how hard she pushed, however, Mrs. Price's moaning still haunted her.

She let the curtains fall back into place. Her stomach grumbled. It was just her, her empty stomach, Mrs. Price and the rifle on her bed.

COCAINE WITH HEART
BY E.M. MACCALLUM

Not many women were attracted to funeral directors, let alone ones that were going under. Business was slow. He found he couldn't compete now-a-days. These new miracle cures and the larger funeral homes throwing out emotionally grim advertisements, he was doomed to fail.

Lenny felt the familiar loathing for his competitors hinder his task. Sighing heavily, he attempted to concentrate. Grinding the dried red flakes in the mortar with the pestle he listened to the familiar scrap of stone. It was almost soothing, like a sound long forgotten from his childhood.

The purple wall-papered room was dimly lit, the casket behind him open containing his only client, Robert Anthony McLean. He had made millions in stocks and bonds, but was dead before he could spend it all.

Luckily for Lenny, Robert McLean hadn't updated his Last Will and Testament to a newer, polished funeral home. He had died unexpectedly of a heart attack while on the can. Much like Lenny's once-idol Elvis Presley, Robert had a high in life before plummeting into Death's greedy hands. It was rather humorous when Lenny gave it a moment to sink in. Dying taking a crap; was there a worse way to go? Lenny could think of few that were as entertaining.

On the counter to his right, Lenny slipped his fingertips into the crinkled plastic bag. Emerging with a white powder, he sprinkled it within the contents of his concoction. Pausing before resuming the monotonous mix, he allowed the muscles in his arms to rest. If given a chance he knew he should buy a chair for the thin mixing table, standing for so long made his legs feel weak.

The sound of the kettle boiling at the small table behind him reminded him of his tea.

He set down his instruments meticulously before shuffling the few feet. He wished he had gotten a younger client than Robert McLean. Each movement of his joints was an anticipation of pain, which rarely failed his expectations.

His knees wobbled when he bent over the tiny table. His favorite chair sat next to it, taunting him. It faced the casket and the only door leading in or out of the tiny parlor. The metal instruments and make-up were laid neatly on the rolling metal tray next to the casket which took up most of the confined space.

With shaky hands, he poured boiling water into his favorite cup that read: "World's Greatest Mortician", a gift from his former assistant. With the tea bag simmering in the water he shuffled back into the other room, careful not to jostle the hot liquid. He had spilled it before in his old age; it was never pleasant to dress up a corpse with blisters on his hands.

Suddenly, the door swung open.

Hadn't I locked it? He wondered in horror, cursing his memory.

Lenny felt his heart stop and he almost sloshed the hot water. Clumsily he was able to shove the cup onto the rolling tray near his embalming tools with a clatter.

The man who burst into his office froze at the same time as Lenny. He was a young chap, well compared to Lenny; he couldn't be older than forty at best. His unruly brown hair nearly stood on end, as if he had rolled out of bed. His thin face was blotchy from hours of tear-spent grief.

Lenny recognized him immediately as Robert's son, Malcolm.

"What the hell?!" Malcolm snapped sending a ripple of anxiety through Lenny's thinning bones. "What the hell did you do to my father?!" He covered his face with his hand in disgust. Not many people enjoyed the smell of formaldehyde, stale air and sterilizers.

Lenny's gray eyes shifted to the corpse. The heavy

cream still covered Robert's face. It was done to preserve the skin. However, Lenny doubted that was what frightened Malcolm McLean.

The chest cavity had been split, hollowed out so that a singular organ was missing, his heart. The blood had been drained leaving much of the man deflated. He was naked from the chest up for the crude surgery.

"You shouldn't be here," Lenny said softly, meekly so not to frighten the young man.

"I think I should," Malcolm erupted, his narrow frame stiffening. Fierce eyes snapped to the old man. "This is against the law. Isn't it? It's against the law!" He accused, pointing his finger and stamping like a disgruntled bull.

"Now, now," Lenny said softly.

Malcolm's eyes scanned the tiny parlor, a place few people other than Lenny and his former assistant had been. Lining the shelves were books on occult practices, ancient civilizations and medical journals. The strange beakers and dried herbs scattered about like a cheap Halloween display was nearest to the door. "I'm going to have to report this," Malcolm's voice cracked, his self-righteous manner morphing into a retreat.

"Now, listen," Lenny continued calmly.

"No!" Malcolm burst hoarsely. "You listen. You just desecrated a corpse – my father. I don't care if you only have six months to live; I'm going to see you in jail before morning." He started for the doorway.

Lenny grabbed the cup of tea and flung it. He didn't have time to think it through, just to act. His shoulder screamed in protest at the sudden movement and he did his best to ignore it.

Malcolm shrieked when the scalding water splashed against his sweater. Staggering back into the room, Malcolm's back hit the wall, jostling the casket. Struggling out of the knitted sweater, he was completely consumed with the pain giving Lenny enough time to get to the door.

Grasping the glass knob not only to shut the door but for balance, he shoved the brass skeleton key into the lock to trap them both into the room.

"Now, listen," Lenny said again pocketing the old key in his tattered cardigan.

Malcolm swung the sweater across the room, the sparsely hairy chest was beat red from the boiling water. Slapping his cooler hands against the burn Malcolm looked up at Lenny horrified.

"I had to do that because you're acting rash," Lenny scolded.

"What the fu-"

Interrupting him, Lenny's meek voice rose to a gargling screech that caused Malcolm McLean to pause. In his youth, Lenny remembered a booming voice that could stop traffic. Frowning, he croaked, "You will refrain from profanities here. This is a place of the dead, you show respect." His throat rattled with the dislodged bile and he began to cough.

"I'll kill you," Malcolm sputtered. "This is not respect. There was no need for an autopsy."

"Course not," Lenny waved a hand at him, covering his mouth with his handkerchief until his fit ceased. "However I'm doing a lengthy process that you wouldn't understand."

"Try me," Malcolm growled in a way that led Lenny to believing that he wouldn't keep an open mind even if Lenny tried to explain how often he withered away, how often he had to replace pieces and his secret tradition of mixing the dehydrated heart and brain of his clients. To absorb bits of former fortitude's was the only thing that kept him alive.

After nearly one-hundred and twenty years on this earth he had to replenish his low supplies, what Death tried to steal from him, he stole from Death. He had long ago dismissed the idea that he was still human. He wasn't sure what he had become anymore. A parasite? A new form of human? A warlock? It was long past his analysis. Unlike most of his company, he managed to cheat death. He wasn't sure for how long, but that was a problem for another day.

During his mental meanderings he hadn't noticed Malcolm push away from the wall. With a burst of speed, Malcolm darted for the door, throwing his entire body-weight – which wasn't much – into the frame.

Lenny wasn't far from the scalpel he used on Robert. It was probably his favorite tool.

When Malcolm couldn't break free through the door he dove for Lenny.

Lenny raised the scalpel, gripping it as tightly as he could and braced himself against the impact.

The blade slipped into Malcolm's stomach like a hot knife into butter. The shock registered on Malcolm's face, their eyes locking just before they knocked away from each other. Malcolm fell to the floor.

Lenny, however, was thrown back into the wall. His grip on the scalpel was slick and he almost lost it when Malcolm jerked away. Lenny's hand was coated in a sticky warmth. He didn't have to look to know what it was.

Righting himself awkwardly, his joints threatened to buckle but luckily didn't fail his attempt to stand again.

He inched towards the mixed concoction. Picking up the mortar, it felt heavy in his hands. The bloody hand-print made the smooth stone slippery and it became awkward as he poured the contents out onto the clear glass plate next to the unruly objects that spread themselves across the counter. Dropping the mortar, it fell to the floor with a clatter, rolling towards the casket.

He didn't bother looking to Malcolm, he knew he wouldn't try and attack him again. A man like Malcolm knew little of pain.

With a stiff piece of paper Lenny lined the red-tinged powder into straight lines.

He had spent much of the evening draining the heart. He had then placed it in his trusty dehydrator. The contraption made his work far simpler than waiting days and dealing with the stench.

"What the hell? Is that coke?" Malcolm gasped, his brown eyes focused on the crinkled clear bag by the discarded mortar.

The cocaine was an aid when it came to inhaling the ground bits of Robert's heart. It made the process of absorbing another person less...abrasive. He hadn't enough time to extract the brain and with Malcolm's spontaneous donation he doubted he would have much sleep tonight. Malcolm was undoubtedly going to meet up with his father far sooner than he had expected.

Placing the hollowed tube at his nostril he inhaled deeply, quickly. It stung at first. The moment it collided with the sinus passages it made his eyes water, but within seconds it all changed. The euphoric wonder of the drug began to sink in as if he had been waiting a lifetime just for a taste.

He had to be careful how often he used it but each time was blissfully welcomed. He imagined absorbed the fading stamina and knowledge of Robert McLean and wanting desperately for it to bond. There wasn't so much strength, in fact he could feel the strain in his chest from Robert's heart problems, but knowledge would be plentiful.

Sitting slowly into his favorite chair at the edge of the room he held the bloodied scalpel in one hand and patted the pocket containing the key with the other.

Whimpering, Malcolm pressed his back against the wall, his eyes shifting from his father to Lenny uneasily. The wound wasn't fatal but Malcolm obviously didn't know that. The fear planted in his eyes made Lenny believe that the man was convinced his death was pending.

Well, it will be, Lenny concluded seriously in his own mind.

He did still need vitality, youth, anything to keep him alive. These dying old men weren't enough to keep him running. At least he may be able to sort through his money problems with this man's intellect for the market.

Unfortunately, Malcolm was still rather old in the grand scheme if it all, his organs wouldn't last Lenny more than a few months. He would need more.

"Malcolm," Lenny said calmly, "do you have any children?"

WALK TOWARDS THE LIGHT
BY JEFFREY A. ANGUS

Red was a simple man who lived a simple life and did not seem to mind. He lived by himself in a little house, what most people would call a shack, near the creek on Styx Lane. He would come to work and go about his business the same way every day. Up at 4am and out the door at 4:15, he would walk to work no matter the weather. His six-foot-five frame and flame red hair made him easy to spot as he crossed the field and made his way through the graveyard to his place of business. Red was the town of Braun's Undertaker/Coroner/Historian. His partner Jim Gregg handled most of the grave work. Red was different than many people in that he liked what he did and it gave him a sense of purpose. He was not fond of change so he looked the part of an undertaker. His dark long coat and stovepipe hat was who he was.

Red removed his hat and ducked to enter the room. He sighed, still not used to the new facility which consisted of two large 12 body fridges, one deep-freeze 3 body freezer and two small 3 body fridges to allow for isolation, if required. Red made his way over to one of the small isolation fridges. He was happy that they had no residents in that section. Red opened the door and a cool cloud of air escaped. He reached in and pulled out a slab. He grabbed a carton of milk and made his way over to the coffee maker. Red always began his day with his cup of coffee and a prayer.

"Lord give them the strength they need to pass over and to see why they lived the life they lived. Forgive those who did not look to the future and only lived in the now. Amen."

Crossing to one of the big storage refrigerators, he swung open the door. On top of the flat he pulled out of the unit was an occupant covered in a white sheet. Red stood and looked at the sheet; a nervous smile on his face. After taking a long draw of his coffee, which he then set aside, he slowly pulled the sheet down so he could see the face of the corpse. The eyes of the dead man were wide open and looked at him.

"Well Mr. Worth, looks like you made it," he said with a sigh of relief.

Red closed the dead man's eyes and kissed Mr. Worth's forehead.

"Soon we can release you to loved ones so they can mourn. I'm glad you made it to your destination."

He covered the corpse back up and pushed the slab back into cold storage. He went to the next square fridge enclosure, opened it, and once again rolled out the slab. The white covered body was on its side.

"Son of a bitch."

With a panic, Red quickly uncovered Mr. Rink. As Red turned him over onto his back, he noticed one of the corpse's eyes was wide open and was a deep blue. Red opened the other eye and it was a dark brown.

"This will not do at all."

Red hurried over to the phone and dialed a number.

He lit up a cigar and puffed and tapped his foot as the phone rang on the other end. An answering machine picked up and Red slammed the phone down. He dialed the number and again it rang. This time a sleepy man picked it up.

"What the hell do you want Red?" Jim Gregg breathed into the phone.

"We got a runner Jim; I need to go get him." Red paused for a response.

"Red, are you sure? We haven't had one in months." Jim's voice was a bit stronger now that he was awake.

"Would I be calling you at this time of the morning if I didn't have to? You're a bitch when you first wake up."

"Kiss my ass Red."

"You just made my point, so I'm going in."

"Last time you almost didn't make it out. Are you sure

you want to do this?"

"We don't have time to argue. I need you here. I'm starting now."

Red slammed the phone down into the receiver and headed towards a work bench in the back of the room. He hastily moved aside the empty bottles and newspapers that covered the stainless steel bench. He pushed down on the top of the flat surface and like magic it slowly slid back into the wall. In the hidden compartment was a locked, ornate suitcase. The carvings on the suitcase depicted pictures of undertakers throughout history. From the traditional stove pipe hats to the more modern, the box was covered on every available inch.

He removed the suitcase and laid it on a nearby counter. From around his neck, he pulled off a chain on which adorned a gold key. He kissed the key and slid it into the lock of the suitcase. Red backed away as the key started to glow. It vibrated and hummed as it turned itself in the lock. With a loud click and hiss, the suitcase opened. And then all was silent except for the humming of the large body fridges.

Red watched the case, waiting to make sure it was done with the opening process. Satisfied that it was, Red approached it. He first pulled out a pair of glasses with thick lenses. He winced as he put them on as they formed to his head, becoming part of his body. Next he grabbed a strange looking device that resembled a pistol. After picking up his final item, a stop watch, he crossed quickly to his desk and scribbled on the notepad…

"Jim, Gone in at 5:35am. Make sure I'm out by 9:00."

He headed back to the slab on which Mr. Rink was stretched out. Opening the door to the occupied fridge next to Mr. Rink, Red hastily pulled out the slab and dumped the body onto the floor.

"Sorry Mrs. Kline, this is an emergency. I'll make it right when I return."

Red climbed onto the slab and took one more look

around. He took the pistol looking device and pointed it at Mr. Rink and fired. A red bolt of energy hit Mr. Rink and his body started to glow.

"That will help me pick you out of a crowd."

He then opened the stop watch and clicked the button; it started to vibrate and a long needle extended out of the back. The needle continued to grow until it was at least a foot long. Red braced himself and jabbed the needle into his chest until the stop watch rested against his skin. His body started to convulse.

Then everything went black.

When Red opened his eyes he stood in a place he had been many times before. The surrounding desert of grey sand had rocks strewn all about. Red looked around to see if he could see any sign of Mr. Rink.

"Yeah, not that easy." His voice echoed and played back to him muffled.

Red started his search, his glasses from the material plane allowed him to see far into the gloom. He could make out the outline shadows and shapes of other souls who had lost their way. Past travelers who had made the trip from the living with no guide to assist them. Many who made the trip would not make it to their destination. The tragic soul whose life was cut short unexpectedly or had been murdered or died without being found and prepared by someone like Red who helped them with the journey. A quick scan did not reveal the one he was looking for.

Red turned and was startled as the visage of a man appeared suddenly in front of him. The soul cocked its head left then right, much like a dog that was curious.

"Where am I? Why am I here?" asked the ghostly visage.

"You need to find the white light. Follow the light."

The soul moved away from Red mumbling, "Walk to the light...walk to the light..."

A little angry, Red yelled, "Why aren't the others preparing the souls?"

Red climbed up on a group of rocks to get a better view. He was hoping to see a red outline, the soul of Mr. Rink that he had outline in the world of the living. He looked in all directions but could see nothing. He decided to head out and used the rock formation as a guide so he didn't end up walking around in circles.

Time meant nothing in Limbo, so he wasn't sure how long he had been searching. It must have been at least thirty minutes but he wasn't concerned. The last time he was in it took him three hours. That almost cost him his life. The Cleaners discovered him and didn't like "his kind" entering their realm and trying to re-direct souls that decided they wanted to go in a different direction. But Red was pretty confident that his presence had not been discovered and it would take the Cleaners a while to figure out he was there. Meanwhile, he had to find Mr. Rink.

Red continued to scan the horizon and to his left noticed something strange in the distance. It looked like a doorway, but it wasn't a bright white light like it should be. He headed towards the anomaly and as he got closer he spotted three Cleaners near the door.

"Shit. They've opened a soul-grabbing portal. I have to stop them."

Red had no more finished his sentence when a Cleaner noticed him. This Cleaner was much larger than Red and was a black and green mist floating above the surface. It looked at Red with its bright amber eyes and Red shivered even from this distance. It shrieked in alarm and the other two charged.

Red dove just in time as a beam of dark death energy shot past him. It hit a wandering soul who was unlucky enough to be in the vicinity. The unearthly sound that came from that poor soul made Red's teeth chatter. The Cleaners, now outraged that they destroyed a soul they could have claimed, continued to advance on Red. Spotting an outcrop that would provide cover, Red made a hasty retreat and took up a position behind it.

The Cleaners advanced and Red decided he had to end this now. He popped up and fired his pistol. The beam of white light hit the Cleaner and it exploded into a ball of black fire. The other two beasts had been waiting for this to happen and they fired off a couple well-aimed shots, hitting Red in the shoulder. Red tumbled backwards. His arm shriveled up, all life gone from it. All he could think of was that it looked like a moldy apricot. His gun had fallen out of sight.

Red lay waiting for the end. The creatures would be on him soon. His weapon flung out of sight; he wasn't sure where. He closed his eyes and waited. He could feel the creatures hovering near, so close he could hear their haunting whispers.

"You are foolish, Undertaker. You do not belong in this realm. This is our territory and now you're going to be trapped in here for eternity."

Why didn't they attack? Why didn't they finish him off?

They want to play with me like a mouse.

The sound of a weapon rang out. It was in the opposite direction from the whispers of the beast. Someone was here! Had Jim sent in another Undertaker to help hunt for the soul maybe? Maybe another Undertaker had entered in search of their own lost soul and had come across the battle. The whispers of the beasts turned from mocking to terror as Red felt the heat from one of the creatures as it exploded in pain. Another shot and more heat! The shrieks died down to the crackle of flames.

Red was afraid to open his eyes. What would help him in this realm? Was it a Redeemer? They never really like the Cleaners. But they would only help so they could devour

Red's soul themselves.

It was silent, as Red lie waiting for the end. He reflected on his life and all he had wanted to do. In the end he was satisfied he had done all he could for the living.

Despite being in pain, Red rolled over to a sitting position. He would face his fate head on.

He lifted his head and scanned the area. He could not believe what was in front of him. He stared slack jawed at the bright orange body of Mr. Rink. In the dead man's glowing hand was his pistol.

"Undertaker, what's going on? Am I dead?"

Red smiled and nodded in response to Mr. Rink's question.

"Holy shit. Then it's true. My brother wasn't full of it."

Mr. Rink dropped the weapon and just hovered in place. Red reached over with his good hand and took the pistol off the ground.

"You are supposed to follow the light." Red clicked a switch on the pistol and aimed it at Mr. Rink.

Pain suddenly shot through Red. He convulsed once, then his world went black.

The stopwatch needle was removed from his chest and Jim Gregg hit him with the charged paddles again. Red's eyes flew open as Jim tried to pull him back from Limbo. Pain and nausea greeted Red, and then his world went black.

The lights in the room assaulted his vision. Red blinked and tried to wipe the focus back to his eyes. He felt a strange numbness all over his body.

"Welcome back to the world of the living," Jim stood next to him, sipping his coffee.

"Jim, is that you?"

"No, it's Saint Peter and it's time for you to polish the

gate," Jim snickered.

"You son of a bitch. I had him. You pulled me out too soon, you stupid ass."

Jim shook his head and smiled. "Well, when your arm went black I was sure it was trouble. I had hoped you had finished but wasn't going to take the chance."

Red managed to sit up. His arm looked more like a sausage than a human appendage. He could move his fingers but it was going to take some time for the bruising to go away and to get full use of it again.

"I had just switched over the weapon to give him a redirection shot and you pulled me out."

Red stood up and looked at Mr. Rinks covered corpse on the table. The glow had faded and now he just lay rigid on the slab. Red slowly stood, his body not fully recovered from his trip. He made his way to the slab that Mr. Rink occupied. He uncovered him; Mr. Rink was now lying flat on his back, both eyes closed. Red looked up at Jim.

"Did you do this?"

"Do what? I got here just in time to get you out safe. Dang funeral going on down the street, held me up a good fifteen minutes. How ironic is that?"

Red looked at Mr. Rink again and smiled. Looks like the dead man's brother did the work for him. Gregg helped him slide Mr. Rink back in to the cooler then walked over to where Mrs. Kline lay on the floor.

"Hey Red, I was going to mention, why Gladys? Not the first thing I wanted to see when I walked in. A pile of naked ninety-six year old Gladys Kline."

"Well it could have been Mrs. Arbuckle."

The two visibly shivered and tucked Gladys back into her cooler. The two men grabbed a cup of coffee and headed out the door.

"We need to train a young gun to help us out in these situations," Gregg patted Red on the back.

"We need to look up Mr. Rink's brother. He might be

able to help."

The doors swung shut behind him and the room was silent, except for a cold hiss and a white mist escaping from the compartment Mrs. Kline occupied.

TAKE THIS JOB AND...
BY SUZANNE ROBB

Nick Holbrook was woken up by incessant ringing. He reached over and slapped his alarm clock, but the noise didn't stop. Opening one eye he looked at the time, it was three in the morning. The ringing started again and he realized it was his cell phone.

"Damn it."

He reached over and answered the phone.

"Holbrook Mortuary, how can I help you at this time?"

"We have a body to drop off. Now."

Nick sighed. Why couldn't people wait until the morning?

"Of course. Whatever I can do to accommodate the family."

Nick thought he heard the guy chuckle but chalked it up to being tired.

Hanging up the phone he got dressed, went downstairs and got the body room ready. He was waiting by the garage when his cell phone rang again.

If they are calling to say they are just gonna come tomorrow so help me...

"Holbrook Mortuary, how can I help you at this time?"

"Be careful when it gets there, embalm it right away."

The connection was severed when the unmarked van pulled up. Two burly men got out and went to the back. Nick heard doors opening, a gurney hitting the ground, and then they reappeared.

"Wheel it in there guys." Nick indicated the room they should take the gurney with the dead body on it.

Lost in thought about the phone call, he was startled when they came out and handed him a clipboard. They waited for him to sign it, showing obvious impatience.

Night crew were never that talkative. This was usually a second job that they slept through. Not him though, he was an undertaker and that meant he worked all the time.

Locking the door behind them he went into the room to see what he was dealing with. All he knew was from a cryptic phone call.

"Be careful when it gets there, embalm it right away."

At first he thought it was a prank. His friends were always doing stuff like that. One time they had sent over an inflatable woman that had a hole in it, with the request that she be embalmed with silicone.

Another time they had snuck in and placed vampire fang veneers on a client. When he saw them he did get a bit scared, but realized he was being set up when he heard them laughing in the hallway. He removed the veneers and tried to explain to them that they could cost him his job pulling crap like that

It didn't stop them; in fact, it seemed to add steam to their effort. It was shortly after that they pulled off their best one to date. One that he was sure they could never top, no matter how outrageous they got.

They had sent one of themselves in. While he was working on another client they got out of the bag and put on a shredded suit and Zombie make-up. Nick had his headphones on and didn't hear what they were doing, but when they tapped his shoulder and he turned around he had the crap scared out of him, literally.

Since that time they had not been around to top themselves. His guess was this was their latest attempt at scaring him. Bracing himself he went through the door and looked at the gurney.

The paperwork was on top and indicated that the body was of a male that died from severe gastrointestinal distress. That was weird; he never had one of those before.

Nick tried to imagine just how severe the distress would have to be to cause one to die. The instructions from the family were simple, drain the blood and embalm. There was one odd request; they wanted to keep the blood that was drained.

Again, that was something new for him. He was starting to think this was his friends up to something. Walking over to the gurney he took a deep breath, bracing himself as he grabbed the zipper and opened the bag.

The smell was horrific. Nick had to actually run to the basin and throw up. In two years of this job that had never happened to him.

What the hell is that smell?

Nick walked back over to the body with a menthol-soaked tissue up his nose. Trying to breathe though his mouth he took a look at the body. The man was bloated and his skin was blotchy. Things were moving around, but that happened on occasion. Gas bubbles, pockets of air, all sorts of things caused dead bodies to appear like they were still moving.

Nick took a closer look and saw that the smell was mainly coming from where he had been sewn up. The skin there was decomposing at a rapid rate. The guy's file indicated he died a few hours ago, but the degree of decomp Nick was seeing was that of someone dead at least a week.

Severe gastrointestinal distress also meant something entirely different to whoever did the paperwork at the hospital. There was obvious distress to the gastrointestinal area, but it looked to Nick as if the abdominal area had been torn open in some way.

It resembled something that had been ravaged. If this was the work of his friends they were getting better. Something about it though just didn't seem right. He let his curiosity get the better of him and decided to investigate this gastrointestinal distress.

Walking over to the instrument tray he picked up a scalpel. It would cut through the stiches with precision and accuracy. Approaching the body he noticed that it was still moving, but he was also still telling himself that bodies do that.

He remembered once when a body had sat straight up, or when one had clenched its hand. One time he even had one that belched for an hour straight. Dead bodies do weird things. He kept that on a repeat loop in his head.

He cut four stiches when he noticed the incision was oozing. That shouldn't be happening. Once the heart stopped beating, the blood stopped flowing. There should be no oozing. He heard a weird raspy noise that sounded like wheezing.

Going into panic mode he thought that perhaps this man might still be alive. He placed his head on the chest, heeding no attention to the ooze that was getting on him. He didn't hear a heartbeat, but that didn't mean anything. It could be too faint for a human ear to detect.

He opened the eyes using his fingers and got another surprise. There were milky and discoloured. This guy was listed as being thirty-eight, with no known vision issues. There was no explanation for the eyes.

Nick took a few calming breaths and decided that tonight would be a good night to take a hit off the bottle of scotch he kept in his desk. Three shots later he returned to the body. It was still moving, but he knew something wasn't quite right.

He felt something drip off his face and remembered he had put his face in that rancid smelling ooze. Running to the eye wash basin he put the side of his face in it. Then he went to the sink and poured bleach on his face and scrubbed with the nearest thing he could find.

Ten minutes later, with only a minor contact-high and some severe abrasions from the steel wool he used to scrub his face, he returned to the body once more.

Scalpel in hand, he cut more stitches. When enough were cut he pulled back the skin and stood slack-jawed at what he saw. The entire gastrointestinal tract was gone, as was the liver, kidneys, most of the stomach, and bits of the lungs.

He looked closer and saw what looked like bite marks, but that had to be wrong. That would mean there was a cannibal on the loose and they would put something like that on the news.

No kidding this guy died from gastrointestinal distress! Talk about an understatement. Having your intestinal tract completely removed would be distressing.

That gave Nick an idea. He went to the paperwork to see what hospital the body came from. If he could talk to the doctor he might be able to get some information.

Not only was there no hospital listed, there was no delivery service, no doctor, and no contact information about the family.

The body was moving again and Nick was starting to worry. What happened to this guy? Did he eat a government secret that resulted in having his internal organs removed? Perhaps he was lactose intolerant and blew up? Maybe he was an alien and the government was trying to cover it up?

Nick went to his desk and took two more shots of scotch. It was close to four in the morning, too late to call anyone that might be able to help him. He was sure his friends weren't behind this because it was far too elaborate for them and creepy if he was being totally honest.

He decided to do what the voice on the phone told him, he was going to embalm it right away. He marched over to the body with the determination of a drunk and admittedly creeped-out undertaker.

Nick rolled the body out of the bag and onto the embalming table. The smell was unbelievable and the body had released some more fluids. Using the hose overhead he rinsed off the feces and urine that encrusted the body.

When that was done he used the plug to stop any more liquids from being spilled via the rectum. Using all his might to turn the man over he felt his arm being grabbed.

Screaming like a little girl and hoping to God his friends were going to run in and start laughing he stood there frozen in fear. After a moment no one ran in, and the hand gripping his arm loosened.

Taking a breath he eased his hand out of the grip of the dead hand. He went to the bathroom, removed his pants, and then peeled off his shorts. He cleaned himself up, put his suit pants back on, and dumped his underwear in the medical waste bin.

Going back to the body he noticed the body was back in its normal position. He wasn't going to let this body get the better of him. He was university educated, and contrary to popular belief Mexico had some great schools for future morticians.

He shut the eyes and reached for the draining spike. He remembered that they wanted the blood that he drained. To hell with them he thought. He stuck the spike in the back of the neck and almost had a heart attack when the eyes of the body shot open.

In school they taught him to use superglue to keep the eyes open for a viewing. Tonight he was going to use superglue to keep those damn eyes shut.

After applying the glue, he noticed that nothing was draining. He pulled out the spike to see if it was clogged or something weird was blocking it. Nothing, he found nothing.

As he was staring at the spike he watched as the body sat up. Then he watched as the body got off the table. The body was wandering aimlessly due to the fact that he had glued its eyes shut.

Nick was wondering if he was drunk or perhaps in a loony bin pretending to be a glass of orange juice. Either way his current mental state was not good.

He knew what it was. A Zombie. He had heard about this kind of thing, but never believed it. He knew he was the only line of defence; then again, he also knew what it took to make a Zombie.

There was the possibility for a potential outbreak, and here he was at ground zero. It was up to him to stop this. He took the spike he was holding and hefted it above his head. He charged the Zombie while screaming and drove it into his head.

Nick watched as it fell to the floor and stopped moving. He thought about what to do next and realized that this was a problem that a match and some gasoline could solve. Covering the body in the flammable liquids from the embalming room he lit a match and tossed it.

He never really liked his job anyways. Perhaps Mexico had some good dental schools.

DEAD CRAZY
BY E.J. TETT

He pushed the needle through her lips, carefully sewing her mouth shut so that the stitching wouldn't be seen. It disturbed some people, what he did. But it had to be done. It was his job.

He tied off the stitch, cut the thread, and placed the needle back onto the metal tray by the table. Mrs. Perkins looked much better now. He just needed to brush and set her hair. The old lady would look good for her funeral; he would make sure of it.

Arthur picked up the brush and hairspray, stood for a moment, deciding where to start, and then got to work.

"Now then, missus," he said, turning the brush through grey curls, "let's make you look beautiful for that old man of yours, eh?"

The clatter of something metallic hitting the floor made him drop the hairbrush. Arthur held a hand to his chest, then relaxed when he saw the cat winding past his pots and jars on the shelf.

"Scared the life out of me, you old rascal," he said, chuckling. He leaned down to pick up the razor which had fallen and put it back on the shelf.

He turned back to see Mrs. Perkins sitting up on the table, wide-eyed and feeling her lips with trembling hands. Arthur's eyes rolled back in his head and he passed out, hitting the floor with a thud.

When Arthur came to, the light above him was flickering. He blinked, groaned, then sat up and rubbed the back of his head. He checked to see if there was blood on his hand and, seeing none, got to his feet.

Mrs. Perkins was lying on the table. Dead. Arthur approached her tentatively, peering at her with suspicious eyes. She was definitely dead.

"Overworked and overtired," Arthur muttered. He checked his watch and saw that it was past midnight. With a sigh, he started work on Mrs. Perkins again, knowing that the funeral was early in the morning and she had to be ready.

He picked up the hairbrush again. "Now then, missus," he said sternly. "Stay dead, there's a good girl."

He worked quickly and once he was done, covered the old lady over with the sheet. He looked at his watch again, checked that the cat was no longer in the room, then turned off the light and closed the door.

It rained in the morning. Arthur stood, water pouring from the brim of his top hat, watching from a distance as relatives threw earth onto Mrs. Perkins' coffin.

Arthur felt a sneeze coming and he quickly took his handkerchief from his top pocket and covered his nose. He hoped he wasn't coming down with a cold. He sniffed, inspected the contents of the kerchief, then placed it back into his pocket.

He watched as the funeral goers started filing back in his direction and he removed his hat respectfully. Family members thanked him and he offered a few quiet words. He waited for them all to leave before putting his hat back on and hurrying to his hearse.

He turned the heater on and dried his hands over it before taking off his top hat and placing it on the passenger seat.

Arthur sighed. "Another one down," he said. He turned the key in the ignition and reversed out of the bay. He promised himself he'd have a nice hot bath as soon as he got home.

He was just putting the car into first gear to drive away when something in the rear view mirror caught his eye.

In the graveyard, standing next to Mrs. Perkins' grave, was a figure dressed all in black. Arthur turned on the rear windscreen wipers to clear the rain from the glass so that he could get a better look, but as soon as the water cleared, the figure had vanished.

Arthur ran a hand over his face. A shiver ran down his spine. He could've sworn the figure was... No. That was silly. The Grim Reaper?

He chuckled and pulled away, driving out of the car park. He was definitely coming down with something, he thought. Probably the flu.

That evening, Arthur was polishing the name plate on a coffin, ignoring the cat winding itself around his ankles.

He stood back and admired his work, when suddenly, he heard a knocking. He looked back towards the mortuary with a frown on his face.

"What's that now, eh?" he asked the cat.

The animal looked up at him and meowed. Arthur tucked his polishing cloth into his pocket and, telling himself that it was nothing, he walked to the mortuary door and pulled it quickly open.

The room was full of people dressed in blue hospital gowns. They turned as one and looked at Arthur. He swore loudly and slammed the door shut, backing up until he bumped into the coffin.

His heart was hammering. The cat came and rubbed itself against his legs as if nothing had happened. Arthur stared at the door.

Eventually he took a deep breath, told himself that he needed to stop being a coward, and went back to the door. If people were up then they weren't really dead and the poor souls were probably frightened and confused.

He opened the door, wincing as it creaked. The mortuary was empty, save for one man laid out on a table covered with a modesty cloth.

"You alright, young man?" Arthur asked. "You're not thinking about getting up and walking around, are you?"

The man was dead. Arthur closed the door and looked back at the cat, now sitting and washing its paws. "I need to get myself to the docs," he said.

He pulled the cloth from his pocket, put it back where it belonged, then left the room and made his way outside. The night was cool and the breeze woke him up. He told himself he was too old for the job; that he tired easily and his mind played tricks on him.

He stretched the kinks from his back and then walked to his car. It wouldn't hurt to see a doctor in the morning. Just in case.

The doctors' waiting room smelled bad. It smelled, Arthur thought, worse than death. It smelled of illness mixed with furniture polish and urine.

Noisy children played with the toys laid out for them in the corner. One man coughed loudly into his hand. A woman, sitting next to Arthur, listened to music far too loudly in her headphones.

Arthur wondered what he would say to the doctor. That he saw dead people? Well, of course he did. It was his job. He frowned and decided he'd just ask for a checkup.

He watched the numbers on the screen and then down at the slip in his hand. It was like being in a supermarket, waiting for service. He sighed and drummed his fingers on his knees.

The girl next to him gave him a glare. He gave her a smile in return and she looked away. The numbers changed again and Arthur got to his feet, heading through the door and down the corridor, looking for his doctor's room.

He went inside when he found it, and took a seat. The doctor spun on her chair, swinging away from the computer screen she had been staring at. She smiled and Arthur offered an explanation for his visit.

He spent the next few minutes having his blood pressure monitored and his weight checked and his urine sampled. He left with the offer of free flu jabs if he wanted them, and a clean bill of health.

When he arrived back home, he couldn't decide whether he felt better or worse.

The poor young girl had been beautiful when she had been alive. She looked different now though, shrunken and ugly.

Arthur took out his pot of moisturiser and spread it over her cheeks, knowing that he had the skills to make her look like she was only sleeping, before wiping his hands on a cloth.

The family had provided him with a photo of the girl when she had been living and he looked at it now before setting the girl's features.

Taking an eye cap from his tray, he prised open the girl's left eye and popped the cap in, before doing the same with the other eye, closing the lids afterwards. He glanced at the photo again briefly, then turned back to the girl.

Her eyes were open. Arthur paused, a frown on his face. He raised a hand to close her lids when her eyeballs moved. She looked at him.

Arthur staggered backwards, knocking into a table behind him. His heart raced as he watched the girl, telling himself that he'd just imagined it. But her head turned slowly and she looked right at him.

Thinking that he might have a heart attack if he stayed there much longer, Arthur turned and hurried out of the room, closing and locking the door with shaking hands. He didn't know whether he should ring the police or the girl's family... or the men in white coats.

He gasped and looked at the door, trying to remember whether the cat had been in the room or not. Then he decided that he didn't care *that* much, and that the cat was perfectly able to look after himself.

He pressed an ear to the door but could hear no movement inside. Dead people were quiet though, he knew that.

"Miss?" he called. If she answered then there'd been a terrible, terrible mistake. Although Arthur had checked himself and she had definitely been dead when he'd started work on her.

She didn't answer. It had to be his imagination; he'd not got round to sewing her lips shut yet. He sighed and took the key from his pocket, putting it into the lock and turning it.

When he opened the door, the girl was just where he'd left her, lying on her back with her eyes closed. Arthur ventured into the room and stopped by the table. "Silly old fool," he told himself. Tentatively, though, he picked up her wrist and felt for a pulse, just in case.

Finding none, he took his needle from the tray and squinted as he tried to thread it.

It continued for weeks. Arthur saw the dead move and

when they were buried, he saw the figure dressed in black. He figured he was crazy, as that was the only logical explanation he could think of, and as the dead did little more than give him a fright, he carried on with his work as normal.

Mr. Vincent McMurray had been a large man in life and in death he was like a beached whale upon Arthur's table. He had been, Arthur suspected, rather inert in life and luckily, was the same in death.

Arthur finished the embalming and was now washing his hands, smiling as the cat leaned over the sink to try to drink the water from the tap. He dried his hands on a towel, turned, and saw Mr. McMurray struggling to sit up.

Arthur raised his eyebrows. "You'll never heave yourself up over that belly, old boy," he said. "Probably best to lie back down and go to sleep."

He folded the towel and draped it over the side of the sink, stroked the cat, and turned back to watch Mr. McMurray. It was almost comical, but Arthur had worked as an undertaker long enough to know when not to laugh.

He waited patiently while Mr. McMurray rolled about and glanced at his watch briefly to check the time as he was getting peckish and he knew the sandwich van would soon pass by. When he looked up again, Mr. McMurray was still.

Arthur covered the body over and then left the room with the cat darting between his legs. He headed outside and stood on the pavement, peering down the road to see if he could spot the van.

What he saw instead gave him a fright. The Grim Reaper stood in the middle of the road, his black robes moving a little in the wind. By his side, his scythe glinted in the sunlight.

Arthur blinked. In the next instant, the Grim Reaper appeared directly in front of him, smelling like soil and formaldehyde.

"Come for McMurray, have you?" Arthur asked. "Bit early, old son, I've not buried him yet."

The Grim Reaper said nothing. Arthur heard bones click and then fall silent. He waited but nothing happened.

"Sandwich van will be here in a minute," he said. "I don't suppose you eat much?"

He didn't get an answer. He wasn't really expecting one. In the distance, he could see the sandwich van turning into the road so he put his hand into his pocket to count his change.

Tyres screeched. Arthur looked up in time to see his cat dive into a hedge and the sandwich van run into the Grim Reaper, sending Death flying over the roof to land in the road behind the van.

Arthur shoved his money back into his pocket. The driver of the van got out, dragging a shaking hand through her hair.

"I nearly hit the cat!" she told Arthur.

"You hit the Grim Reaper," Arthur replied, looking at the piles of rags in the road.

"The cat? Oh God, I didn't, did I? I thought he ran!"

Arthur headed behind the van and gave the rags a nudge with his foot. The woman joined him. "Oh thank God!" she said, holding a hand to her chest. She gave a little laugh of relief and put her hand to Arthur's arm. "It's just some old clothes. Scared me half to death!"

Arthur reminded himself that he was crazy and that he hadn't really witnessed the sandwich van running over the Grim Reaper. He smiled. "Me an' all," he agreed.

He ordered a tuna sandwich, made sure that the woman was all right, and then watched her drive away. With the sandwich in one hand, he retrieved the Grim Reaper's robe with the other, and went to sit on the bench in the park outside of the funeral parlour.

As Arthur ate his tuna sandwich and watched a mother pushing her child on the swings, he pondered who would help the dead now. He supposed he'd have to do it.

People called him the Grim Reaper. And now he was.

THEY KNOW
BY SHELLS WALTER

It started one day; the cold sweats, the waking up in the middle of the night. Ryan couldn't shake the headaches. The headaches that started once his father died and he inherited the family business, the funeral home. He dreaded going there when he was a teenager and now years later he was the owner.

He had watched his father put make-up on the dead people. It made Ryan feel disgusted. Yet even with all the work he watched his father do, a certain interest started to brew in the money aspect of the business. The people would come in to the funeral home request arrangements for their loved ones and pay the costs. Ryan soon discovered that funeral costs were high. When he took over the funeral home he made a choice to make money from death an easier way, killing them himself instead of waiting for the corpses to come to him.

The first killing was not as hard as Ryan had thought. It was really a simple situation. He waited as the young woman walked down the street. It was dark and she was alone. He came from behind her and slit her throat, took her bag and made it look like a robbery gone wrong. No one had suspected Ryan.

In the city where he slit the woman's throat, bad things always happened. Soon enough the body was looked over for any evidence and then sent to Ryan's funeral home. The family paid big bucks to have her made over and make the necessary arrangements for the huge funeral that would follow.

It was this first killing that Ryan felt his headaches go away. It was also where he had figured it was so simple that he would pursue future victims. The money was so much that he made a choice to hire an assistant. One that would have no clue how the money was made. It was really for professional purposes to show the community he did not work alone.

He found Lina one day at a bookstore. She was looking at books that dealt with death. Soon after he met her, they sat down at the café part of the store and talked. He found out she always wanted to be a funeral director. Ryan found that odd for anyone to want, especially a woman. He invited her to work with him and she had been with him ever since.

They had worked well together. She learned everything from Ryan and when there were new techniques to be learned, she would be the first to go to the conventions. Lina was always excited to share the new information with Ryan who simply nodded and went back to prepping whatever dead person he was working on at the time.

She then would come in at night even with some strange friends she had met. Ryan always watched these friends of hers come in with their weird necklaces and books that they always wrote on when they were in the funeral home. Ryan eventually asked her not to bring them anymore. Lina reluctantly agreed and they never showed up again. It was after that time that Ryan started to notice Lina going off more on her own, doing things in private, but there was never a reason to mistrust her.

He walked the cold cement floor. Ryan sighed and opened the big steel door that entered into the room where he prepared the dead bodies. A job in itself he found disturbing.

Ryan moved his neck side to side and put on his plastic coat as to not get anything on his clothes. He hated the times when he first started. All the garbage that would come at him, spraying out of the dead bodies, ruining his expensive suits. Ryan had learned quickly to use the plastic gear every other

Funeral Director wore. In this particular case, he wore the plastic suit only as a formality as one of his assistants had already embalmed the woman, which was one of the things Ryan hated the most.

The corpse was flat on the metal table in front of him. He took the make-up kit on the counter next to the table. Ryan smacked his lips and swallowed hard trying to keep the disgusting taste that came from his stomach as he looked at the dead body. The woman was ugly, and he thought even uglier upon death. Why did he have to do this? There was no way he could make this woman look any better.

He started with a foundation that gave the ash-colored woman some more life to her face. She stared at him with an intense focus that only the dead could have. Ryan took his right index finger and shut her eyelids. He couldn't take her staring at him as if it was his fault she was dead. She deserved everything she got and then some.

Her family, mostly just her mother and her sister, would be in soon to view her and give Ryan the clothes he needed to dress her for the funeral. He hated the families, always crying and wanting him to make up for their loss. To hell with them! It was their money he enjoyed the most; the feel of the new suits he bought with their grieving dimes. Ryan would put on the act of the concerned person, the one who wanted to help while deep inside he wanted nothing more than for them to join their loved ones.

Ryan finished the make-up on the dead woman and stood back. It seemed okay. He didn't really smooth out anything, but mostly packed on the make-up. The woman looked more like a clown than the classy pianist she was supposed to be. He grinned. They would accept anything he did for them. He was the Master.

He turned around to walk to the sink to wash his hands; of all times he had forgotten to wear his gloves. He cursed as the water hit his manicured hands.

"Not nice to swear young man."

Ryan turned quickly dropping the bar of soap on the floor. He rubbed his eyes.

"What the…" Ryan took a step back.

"What's wrong, you never seen a dead body before? I thought you worked here?" The woman smiled a somewhat toothless grin.

Ryan knew in the past few days sleep was something of a pastime. He knew he must have been seeing things. The woman sat up, parts of her not fully attached, so half her body went lopsided. An arm barely hung on to her body. It swayed as she started to get up. The accident she was in severed many parts of her body. Ryan had thought his assistant had put together any limbs that were torn apart. He reminded himself, even in his current state of fear, to yell at his assistant.

"I know what you're thinking," the dead woman said as she moved closer to him. Ryan stepped back further and tried to maintain his balance.

"You're dead," Ryan whispered.

"Am I?" The woman laughed. She inched closer to Ryan, arms looking as if she was flying, they were flapping so much.

Ryan didn't understand. He saw the woman dead on the table. He had just finished her make-up.

"What do you want from me?" Ryan had now pinned himself against the large door behind him.

"Don't you know young man?"

Ryan's eyes widened. Of all days for him to miss a date with Jerry, to come here and make sure she was done, and now this.

"Don't you like me?" The woman took one of her half-attached arms and tried to rub down her other arm, showing Ryan what she was like.

He watched as she moved closer. Her body was decomposing right in front of his eyes and confusion set in. He couldn't figure out how she could be decomposing so quickly. It was impossible! He had prepared so many dead bodies before. How could one be messed up like this, or better yet, how is it that she was moving?

"I don't understand what you want from me." Ryan started shaking.

"My dear, you should know. I've heard you."

Ryan looked around. "Heard what?"

"Your thoughts."

Ryan swallowed hard. He could feel everything he had eaten starting to come up.

"I don't know what you mean," Ryan said slowly.

"All you want is money for us, don't you?" The woman almost slid across the floor. Her feet dragged behind her in a most distorted way. Ryan shook his head no.

"Now, now. Is it nice to lie to your elders?" She was almost to where Ryan was standing. He turned quickly to open the door, but it was jammed. He tried jerking it free. It wouldn't budge.

Ryan turned back slightly to see the woman still approaching.

"Why me?!" He screamed.

"Why you? You're the one that takes our lives, turns them around and for what, so that you can kill us later to retrieve your money?" The woman's eyes dead from all life looked hollow and black with anger.

"No, I give you your life back. I give your loved ones a sense of comfort," Ryan pleaded.

"And how much does this comfort cost?" The woman spoke and lost a couple of her decomposed teeth. Her eyes started to fill with ooze that dripped down her cheeks. Ryan gagged.

Ryan could feel his heart racing. He looked over to his right and saw three more corpses stumbling toward him. Two men and one woman decomposed beyond recognition; maggots had already buried themselves in any opening on their bodies. Ryan screamed, turned around and pounded on the door with his fists.

"Let me out!" He had hoped his assistant was still there. She should still be on her shift, yet still there was no one that answered the door.

The pianist and three other corpses were right at Ryan. He turned just in time to see all four attack him. They tore at his plastic jacket, ripping it apart. They started chewing at his flesh, ripping it off in pieces. The old woman pushed her hand into Ryan's chest. Blood spurted everywhere as Ryan slid to the floor.

Lina unlocked the door leading to the preparation room. As the door opened it pushed against Ryan's dead body. She looked down at his corpse and smiled. The reanimated dead who had chewed away at his body were gone. The window in back was smashed where they had made their exit into the world of the living.

Lina set down the brown folder she was carrying under her arm and opened it. Inside contained paperwork and journal entries that told how each client was searched out, killed and their families contacted for funeral arrangements. Ryan had personally killed all these people just to make more money off of them.

It was only on the second day of her employment that she'd found the folder and immediately recognized the photo of the first victim --- her sister. Because her sister was married and had a different last name, Ryan never knew he'd hired his first victim's kin. And Lina never brought it up as the pain of her senseless death at the hands of an unknown mugger was too much for her to bear.

In light of this recent discovery, she vowed revenge and decided to use the new formula she'd created with the help of her friends that dabbled in the black arts. When Ryan allowed her to embalm these particular corpses herself, she saw her opportunity! And it turned out perfectly! The dead rose again and would take care of people like Ryan.

She looked at Ryan's torn body. It pleased her to think that she'd finally avenged her sister's murder. Lina took the folder off the table and threw it on the floor next to Ryan. If anyone came into this place ever again they would find him with the folder. She hoped that he would just rot in this room like those rotting corpses that were now among the living.

POSSESSION IS NINE-TENTHS OF THE LAW
BY STEPHANIE K. DEAL

"Hi honey. I should be home on time tonight. I've got one last body to process. Shouldn't take too long. The Burns kid...No, this is the seventeen-year-old kid that went head-first off the end of a skateboard ramp into the outlet. The car accident was Anthony Morelli's son. He's being laid out at Peaceful Pines Funeral Home across town...Yeah. Do you need me to stop at the store for anything?...Eggs and Rotini pasta, sure. See you about six...Love you too. Bye."

Dr. Michael Billingsley closed his cell phone and set it on his desk then crossed the room to his last guest of the day. He preferred to call the bodies brought to him as guests. He welcomed them, cared for them and they left looking a lot better than when they arrived. His embalming room was a spa for the dead.

"Mr. Burns," Michael looked down at the kid on the embalming table. "Why in the hell didn't you wear a helmet? I know. I know. You don't look nearly as cool wearing a helmet. But you wouldn't look nearly as dead now if you had. Right? Right?! Getting thru to you kids is impossible."

Huh? Where the hell am I? Am I in the hospital? Looks like that bastard Joey was right again. That stunt was stupid. Probably busted up my arm and another skateboard. Again. It's awful damn bright in here. Am I lying on a table? What kind of hospital is this? Can't they even put me in a bed? Shit. Well, here's the doctor. Hopefully he'll just give me some good drugs and I can ditch this place. What in the hell is in his hand? Is that a saw? Holy shit! That's a saw! What are you going to do with that saw?! Hello?!? Dude! Are you even listening to me?!? Oh my god!!! Why

doesn't that hurt?!? What kind of drugs did you give me?!? I gotta get out of here! SHIT!!!

A wave of pain flashed thru Michael's head.

"Shit."

He stumbled back, grabbing his head and dropping the saw. Thankfully the safety shut it off as soon as it left his hand. The pain passed as quickly as it came and he picked up the saw.

"That was weird."

He looked down at the Burns kid. He'd accidently sawn thru the top of the ear.

"I can fix that."

Nausea started to set in as he examined the extent of the damage.

"Get a grip Michael. You're not in fucking med school anymore. Let's just finish this."

He pushed the nausea back and continued to work. Within forty-five minutes he was done, Burns was in the cooler and he was washed up and heading for the store.

"Babe! I'm home!"

"Hi. Did you remember to stop at the store?"

He dropped ten grocery bags on the kitchen table.

"I guess you did," she started going thru the bags.

"I couldn't remember what pasta you said, so I got one of each."

"Ok. I guess that works," she side-eyed him. "And the two bags of frozen pizza, Ho-Ho's and Yoohoo's?"

Michael shrugged. "I don't know. I had a craving."

"You do know none of this food is on your diet. I mean, I don't personally care what you buy or eat but you were pretty insistent that you wanted to stick to — "

She stopped abruptly and stared at him.

"What are you doing?"

"What?"

"Why are you grabbing my boob?"

"Because I can," he grinned. "Mine."

"Have you been sniffing the embalming fluid?"

He squeezed her left breast twice, then winked at her.

"Oh, for crying out loud."

She swatted his hand away while trying to hide her own smirk.

"I have to finish dinner. Put your snacks away please."

He shoved the boxes haphazardly into the freezer and cupboards.

"Done, Babe."

He winked to her once more before leaving the kitchen.

"Babe," she sighed, shaking her head. "What the hell's gotten into you, Michael Billingsley?"

The next day at Crandle Funeral Home Michael prepared to process his next guest. Mabel Paulson. Two days short of her ninety-third birthday her heart finally gave way.

"Good afternoon Mrs. Paulson. My name is Mr. Billingsley and I'll be your spa therapist this afternoon. Let's see just what shape we're in today."

He unzipped the bag and opened it wide to reveal the naked, elderly woman. Michael immediately doubled-over. Crawling back to his desk, he pulled himself into the chair. He grabbed the trashcan to have handy in case he got sick.

The elderly were Crandle's biggest population. He processed at least five bodies a week and at least four of those were people long past the retirement age. Never has it bothered him as it has today. This is the reaction he'd have expected from an intern or med school student. Not from an undertaker with over ten years of experience.

He looked over at Mrs. Paulson's body lying on the table.

"See. It's just a sweet old lady. No biggie."

He passed out.

"I don't know Barbara. Maybe it's just a phase."

"A phase?! We already went thru this phase with him in college. It was kind of cute at first, calling me Babe, pinching my butt, but after two weeks it's getting to be annoying. And now he's bought a mountain bike!"

"Lots of guys buy mountain bikes for exercise."

"He rides it in the junkyard. Says it's more fun."

"Ew. Does he wear a helmet at least?"

"Yes. He said he doesn't want to make that mistake twice. Lord knows what happened the first time. I didn't ask."

"Just as well. I think he's just re-living his youth one more time before you start a family. You guys did talk about that, right?"

"Yeah. We want to have a baby next year. He seemed as excited as I am about it."

"And I'm sure he is. Don't worry about it. Bob did the same thing last year when he turned forty. Out of the blue just started collecting comic books and trading cards. Trust me, junkyard biking is a much better and less expensive hobby."

"Until he breaks his neck."

"Michael's not an idiot like Bob. He'll be fine. Give it another week and it'll run its course."

"It better have. Because it's starting to affect his work."

"His work?"

"He's starting to have headaches at work. Migraines. He came home early three days last week."

"Really?"

"He should get his brain scanned. There's something loose up there. Maybe a tumor."

"Paula!"

"A benign tumor."

"First you tell me it's nothing and now he's got tumors?!"

"Maybe he picked up something at work. He has to work with chemicals all day long. Or maybe something from...you know."

"Know what?"

She whispered into the phone. "A dead person."

"Oh my god," Barbara sighed. "I don't know why I even ask you anymore."

"I don't either, quite frankly. Look, I have to go. The kids are screaming for dinner."

"For what it's worth, thanks for listening to me Sis."

"Anytime."

Barbara hung up.

"Catch something from a dead person," she scoffed, then made the mistake of thinking about it.

"Michael!"

She went out to the garage where he'd said he was going to work on his bike, except he was staring at the box with the unconstructed crib in it. They'd found it on sale. That was three months ago.

"Do you think it's bad luck to put it together now?" Michael asked. "Before we're pregnant?"

"No. I don't believe in bad luck. Just unfortunate circumstances. It's probably best to keep it in the box though until the room is done."

"Yeah," he sighed. "I guess you're right. John called."

"My brother?"

He nodded. "He can't go to the Pearl Jam concert tomorrow."

"Oh no. You've been looking forward to this for weeks. Why not?"

"John Jr.'s baseball team made the tournament finals. He can't miss it."

"That's too bad. Maybe Frank can go with you. He wasn't one of your frat brothers but you hung out with him in college. That's kind of like old-times."

"Why don't you come with me?"

"Me?"

He walked up to her and wrapped his arms around her waist, pulling her closer.

"Yeah. You used to be a huge Eddie Vedder fan."

"That was years ago."

"Come on. You said yourself the other day he still looked good."

She shrugged.

"Remember the first time we went to a Pearl Jam concert? Remember what you did?"

"Yes," she grumbled.

"You flashed the stage."

"I remember."

"Then threw up on my shoes."

"I remember," she stressed.

"I thought you were cute."

"Cute? I was drunk."

He shrugged. "Not that part, necessarily, but you were adorable. You're still adorable."

She started to blush.

"Come on. For old time sake."

"Ok," she relented.

"Awesome Babe!"

He hoisted her over his shoulder.

"Ah! Michael! Put me down!"

"No way. You're mine!"
"Put me down! I'm gonna be sick!"
"Let's go practice makin' babies!"
"MICHAEL!!!!"

"I can't believe you threw up on my shoes again!!"
"I warned you!! You didn't put me down!!"
They stood close to the stage, near the edge of the mosh pit, screaming over the music and crowd.
"And you didn't even flash me first!!"
She rolled her eyes.
"Ok!! I'm going in!!"
"What?!?!"
"Babe!!"
He winked to her and then threw himself into the mosh pit.
"What the hell are you doing?! Are you insane?!"
But it was useless; he was already swallowed up by the crowd of metalheads.
"He's gonna get himself killed."
Michael didn't really care about the mosh pit itself. He wanted one thing. One thing that he'd never done in all the years of coming to concerts.
"Crowd surf!!"
He was hoisted over the center of the pit and passed from one edge to the other.
"WOO HOO!!"
As he neared the front of the stage, someone stumbled and the wave collapsed. Michael was tossed forward over the security barrier and headlong into the front of the stage. Pearl Jam was between songs so lead singer Eddie Vedder took the opportunity to step forward and look down on the fallen crowd surfer.

"Shit," he commented and held his head in sympathetic pain.

Security stood Michael up. Normally they would have tossed him back into the crowd or out altogether, but they were surprised to find him older than your normal crowd surfer.

"You ok sir?!"

Michael rubbed his head.

"Yeah!! I'm too old for this shit!!" he pointed to the far side of the security barrier. "My wife's waiting for me!! Can I leave?!"

"Certainly!!"

They escorted Michael along the barrier until he was to the far edge where Barbara had elbowed her way to the front to check on her husband.

"Michael!! Oh my god!! Are you ok?!"

"I'm fine!! Do you mind if we leave though?!"

"Really?!"

"Yeah!! It's too loud!! And I have to go to the Funeral Home early tomorrow!! I've got a lot of work to make up!!"

"Are you sure?! You've been looking forward to this for weeks!! What about re-living your youth?!"

"I think I've gotten it out of my system now!!"

Barbara smiled; glad to see her husband was back. She hugged him tight.

"Let's go home and practice making babies."

He smiled down at her, wrapped his arm around her waist and they headed towards the exit.

Meanwhile on stage Eddie shouted out.

"Are you ready to rock?! Let me hear you, Dudes and Babes!!! Rawr!!!!!"

He threw the horns with both hands. Guitarist Mike McCready stared at him.

"What the hell's gotten into you?"

ABOUT THE AUTHORS

Jeff Angus lives in Upstate New York with his wife Bonny. He loves to craft stories of all kinds. You can find his work in Strange Tales of Horror and Look What I found published by NorGus Press.

Alex Azar is an author born and raised in New Jersey. He hates the term 'aspiring author' preferring 'struggling author'.

Jennifer L. Barnes lives in New Albany, IN with her insanely patient and geeky husband and perhaps the world's most ungraceful cat. She has an unhealthy obsession with things that go Bump In the Night and has been writing about them since childhood. Jennifer can be reached at writerjennbarnes@gmail.com and would love to hear from her readers.

Jim Bronyaur lives in Pennsylvania and has been published in many anthologies including End of Days (volume 4), Inner Fears, Twisted Tongue, and Diamonds in the Rough. Other stories have been published in Flashes in the Dark, Twisted Dreams, Pow! Fast Flash Fiction, among many others. He doesn't sleep, drinks lots of coffee, and listens to Guns 'n Roses. Jim's web site is www.JimBronyaur.com.

Liam Cadey lives in Bristol, England and has recently decided to walk the long and winding road of writing in his favourite genre, rather than just reading it. Having found it to be a perilous yet pleasurable journey, he intends to get a good pair of writing gloves and begin his quest in earnest…

Jason Countryman once squoze the Charmin. Hard. The chickens have regarded him in awe ever since.

Stephanie Deal considers herself to be the luckiest person in the world to be named as one of the editors for this anthology. She is very proud of the work these authors have submitted. "Thank you Stacey! It has been a complete joy and riot working on this with you. Bitches rule!"

Emma Ennis hails from Ireland – the land of poets and scholars, leprechauns and legends. She currently lives in Norway but frequently returns to her beloved home for some fantastical inspiration. Recently she has had numerous stories published in different anthologies, achieving a lifelong dream. Her all-time goal is to learn how to freeze time so she can read every book that was ever written.

Growing up in a small farming community, **E.M. MacCallum** often spent her free time making up macabre stories. It didn't take much to convince her that writing would be her life's passion. Just beginning her publishing journey she's the author of a few short stories and the upcoming novella "Zombie-Killer Bill" out mid-2011.

Unlike most people, **Nick Medina** goes to sleep each night hoping for bad dreams; they're the inspiration for most of his work. Nick is a young author from Chicago, Illinois. Since seeking publication in 2009, he has been published in print, online and audio formats by magazines, journals and short story anthologies in the United States and the United Kingdom. To read more of Nick's work, or to contact him with questions and comments, visit: http://sites.google.com/site/nickjmedina/

Mike Mitchell is a film maker that has yet to make his film, amateur author and co-host of Don't Look in the Podcast. He currently lives in Terre Haute, Indiana and works in TV production.

Jonathan Moon is a horrorcore author living in the Palouse region of Washington/Idaho. He is the author of Mr. Moon's Nightmares (from Library of Horror Press), HEINOUS (coming 2011 from May December Publications), Co-Author of The Apocalypse and Satan's Glory Hole, with Timothy W. Long (also, from Library of Horror Press), as well as the editor of Houdini Gut Punch: A Bizarro Horror Anthology (yet again Library of Horror Press).

Golda Mowe is a writer from Sarawak, Malaysia who writes flash fiction and short stories. Though she studied Commerce and Accounting, her first love has always been history, myths and folklores, which she continues to explore in her writing.

Matt Nord lives in Central New York with his wife, Karen, and two sons, Jacob and Judah, and little princess Jordan. He is a fledgling horror writer with several credits under his proverbial belt, including several short stories published by Living Dead Press and Library of the Living Dead Press as well as stories to be featured future anthologies from Pill Hill Press, Wicked East Press and Static Movement Imprint. He is also senior editor of the new small press publisher NorGus Press. His most ambitious project to date may be the collaborative novel he is currently spearheading with 18 other authors, and will hopefully see published before his baby daughter graduates college.

Suzanne Robb has stories in current and upcoming anthologies. For Pill Hill Press stories in Daily Flash 2012, Daily Frights 2012, and E-pocalypse; Static Movement anthologies, Monk Punk, Halloween Frights V.II., Shadows Within Shadows 2, After the End, Bounty Hunter, Best Left Buried, Unquiet Earth, and Road Trip; for Library of the Living Dead Press, Rapid Decomposition – Living Dead Flash Stories, Live and Let Undead, and Attack of the 50ft Book; Tales of the Dead – A Zombie anthology for Living Dead Press; a story in the NorGus Press anthology Look What I Found; and stories in Panic Presses' Deadication and Soup of Souls. She is also a member of Collaboration of the Dead, a novel being written by several writers, each contributing a chapter or two.

This is **DC Scharoun's** first foray into writing for the dark side. DC works as a technical support specialist in Auburn for a family-owned company offering last rites to broken printers. DC lives with his wonderful wife and 3 cats in a Victorian fixer- upper thankfully near the ER.

D.G. Sutter is a writer of dark tales and fantastical adventures. He lives with his wife in Western Massachusetts and works in a bookstore. When not writing, he can typically be found curled up on the couch with a cup of joe and a good book.

E.J. Tett is the author of fantasy novel The Kingdom of Malinas, and co-author of horror anthology Casting Shadows. She has appeared in Aphelion, The Horror Zine, Everyday Weirdness and Short-Story.Me. She lives in Somerset, England with her family. Mostly, she dreams of zombies.

Shells Walter has loved horror since she was young. Her work has appeared in several ezines, magazines and has had novellas, novels published as well. She currently writes everything from short stories to screenplays. Upcoming works involve a Horror collaboration novella set from Wicked East Press, an anthology from Wicked East Press that includes some of her short stories with other authors and another Horror Novel in 2011. She can be reached at www.shellswalter.com.